RYAN'S PLACE

Center Point
Large Print

Also by Sherryl Woods
and available from Center Point Large Print:

Dream Mender

Chesapeake Shores Series
The Inn at Eagle Point
Flowers on Main
Harbor Lights

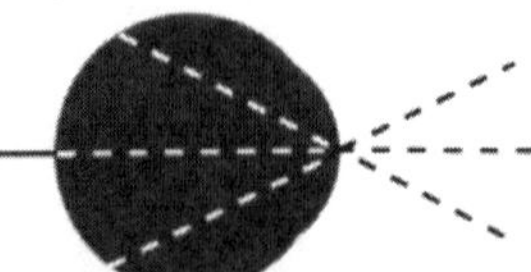

This Large Print Book carries the Seal of Approval of N.A.V.H.

RYAN'S PLACE

SHERRYL WOODS

CENTER POINT PUBLISHING
THORNDIKE, MAINE

This Center Point Large Print edition
is published in the year 2010 by arrangement with
Harlequin Books S.A.

All characters in this book have no existence outside the imagination of the author and have no relation whatsoever to anyone bearing the same name or names. They are not even distantly inspired by any individual known or unknown to the author, and all incidents are pure invention.

The text of this Large Print edition is unabridged.
In other aspects, this book may vary
from the original edition.
Printed in the United States of America
on permanent paper.
Set in 16-point Times New Roman type.

ISBN: 978-1-60285-708-7

Library of Congress Cataloging-in-Publication Data

Woods, Sherryl.
Ryan's place / Sherryl Woods. -- Center Point large print ed.
p. cm.
Originally published: New York : Harlequin, 2002.
ISBN 978-1-60285-708-7 (library binding : alk. paper)
1. Large type books. I. Title.
PS3573.O6418R93 2010
813'.54--dc22
2009049502

RYAN'S PLACE

Chapter One

Ryan Devaney hated holidays. Not only were they lousy for business, but the few people who did walk into his Boston pub were usually just about as depressed as he was. The jukebox tended to blast out its most soulful tunes, which might have reduced him to tears if he hadn't given up shedding them a long time ago. Thanksgiving, with its bittersweet memories, had always been worst of all. And this year promised to be no different.

Outside there was the scent of snow in the crisp air, and back in Ryan's kitchen, his cook was already baking the dozens of pumpkin pies Ryan would be taking to the homeless shelter and also serving to the handful of people who showed up at the pub for a lonely meal tomorrow. Ryan had a very dim recollection of a time when both aromas would have stirred happy memories, but those days were long gone. It had been more than twenty years since he'd had anything at all for which to be thankful.

Even as the thought crossed his mind, he brought himself up short. Father Francis—the priest who evidently considered saving Ryan's soul his personal mission—would blister him with a disapproving lecture if he ever heard him say such a thing aloud. The priest, whose church was just down the block and whose parish benefitted from Ryan's generosity, had a very low opinion of Ryan's tendency to wallow in self-pity around holidays.

"You have a roof over your head. You have money in your pocket and warm food in your belly," Father Francis had chided on more than one occasion, disappointment clouding his gaze. "You have a business that prospers and customers who rely on you. You have countless others who depend on you for food and shelter, though they don't know it. How can you say there are no blessings in your life? I'm ashamed of you, Ryan Devaney. Truly ashamed."

As if Ryan had conjured him up just then, Father Francis slid onto an empty stool at the busy bar and gave Ryan his usual perceptive once-over. "Indulging again, I see."

Ryan winced at the disapproving tone. "Haven't touched a drop," he said, knowing perfectly well that liquor was the last concern on the priest's mind.

"Ah, Ryan, my boy, do you honestly believe you can get away with trying that one on me?"

Ryan grinned at the white-haired man, who still had a hint of Ireland in his voice. "It was worth a try. What can I get you on this chilly night?"

"Would a cup of Irish coffee be too much trouble? The wind is whipping out there, and my old bones can't take it the way they once did."

“For you, Father, nothing is too much trouble,” Ryan told him with total sincerity. As annoying as he sometimes found the priest, Ryan owed him his life. Father Francis had snatched him out of the depths of despair and trouble many years ago and set him on a path that had landed him here, operating his own business, rather than sitting in a jail cell. “Why aren’t you home in front of a fire?”

“I’ve been to visit the shelter. We’ve a new family in there tonight. Can you imagine anything sadder than being forced to go to a homeless shelter for the first time on Thanksgiving eve, when everyone else is fixing turkey and baking pies and preparing to count their blessings?”

Ryan gave him a sharp look. It had been Thanksgiving eve, seventeen years ago, when Father Francis had taken him to the St. Mary’s shelter, scared and hungry and totally alone. Just fifteen, Ryan had been angry at the world and had barely managed to escape being arrested for shoplifting, thanks to the priest’s influence with the local police precinct and the outraged shop owner.

“No, I can’t imagine anything sadder,” he said tersely. “As you well know. What do you want?”

Father Francis smiled, a twinkle in his eye. “Not so very much. Will you talk to them tomorrow? Your own story is an inspiration to many in the neighborhood. Hearing what you've accomplished under difficult circumstances will give them a reason to hope."

"I imagine you think I can find work for at least one of them, as well," Ryan said with a note of resignation in his voice.

There had been a time when he'd had a formal business plan for his pub, complete with goals and bottom-line projections. Taking in Father Francis's strays had pretty much thrown that plan into chaos, but if the priest had asked him to cater a funeral in hell, he would have found some way to do it. Hopefully, this latest request would require less drastic action.

"Well?" he prodded.

"One . . . or both. The fact of the matter is, I understand the mother is a wonderful cook. Didn't you tell me that you're short-staffed in the kitchen?" Father Francis inquired innocently. Before Ryan could reply, he rushed on, "And with the holiday season coming on, you'll be busier than ever in here as folks gather to warm up a bit after their shopping. And some of the local businesses like to use your back room for their Christmas parties, isn't that right? Perhaps you could use another waiter, at least through New Year's."

Ryan cursed his loose tongue. He was going to have to remember that Father Francis was a sneaky, devious man, always looking to pair up his strays with people who casually remarked on some need or another. There had been one point when half his waitresses had been unwed mothers-to-be. For a brief time, he'd been certain his private dining room was going to wind up as a nursery, but even Father Francis had stopped short of making that request. The priest's grudging acknowledgment that a pub was no place for infant day care suggested, however, that the thought had crossed his mind.

"Hiring an extra waiter is no problem. As for the woman, can she fix corned beef and cabbage, Irish stew, soda bread?" Ryan asked.

The priest looked vaguely uncomfortable. "Isn't it time for a bit of a change?" He pulled the bright-green, laminated menu from its rack on the counter and pointed out the entrées that had been the same since the opening on St. Patrick's Day eight years ago. Even the daily specials had remained constant. "It's a bit boring, don't you think?"

"This is an Irish pub," Ryan reminded him dryly. "And my customers like knowing they can count on having fish and chips on Fridays and stew on Saturdays."

"But people eventually tire of eating the same old things. Perhaps a little spice would liven things up."

Spice? Ryan studied him warily. "What exactly can this woman cook?"

The priest's expression brightened. "I understand her enchiladas are outstanding," he reported enthusiastically.

Ryan frowned. "Let me get this straight. You're asking me to hire someone to cook Mexican food in my Irish pub?"

He shuddered when he considered how his born-in-Dublin cook was likely to take to that news. Rory O'Malley was going to be slamming pots and pans around for a month, assuming he didn't simply walk off the job. Rory, with his thick Irish brogue and a belly the size of Santa's thanks to his fondness for ale, had a kind heart, but he could throw a tantrum better than any temperamental French chef. Because his kitchen had never run more smoothly, Ryan tried his best to stay out of Rory's way and to do nothing to offend him.

The priest plastered an upbeat expression on his face. "Ryan's Place will become the most talked-about restaurant in the city, a fine example of our melting pot culture."

"Save it," Ryan muttered, his already sour mood sinking even lower, because despite the absurdity and the threat of a rebellion in the kitchen, he was going to do as he'd been asked to do. "Send her in day after tomorrow, but she'd better be a quick learner. I am not serving tacos in this place, and that's that. Does she at least speak English?"

"Enough," Father Francis said.

He spoke with the kind of poker face that had Ryan groaning. "I should let you be the one to explain all this to Rory," Ryan grumbled.

"Rory's a fine Irish lad and a recent immigrant himself," Father Francis declared optimistically. "I'm sure he'll be agreeable enough when he knows all the facts. And surely he'll see the benefit in the positive reviews likely to come his way."

"On the off chance he doesn't take the news as well as you're predicting, I sincerely hope you can find your way around a kitchen, Father, because I have an apron back there with your name on it."

"Let's pray it doesn't come to that," the priest said with an uncharacteristic frown. "If it weren't for Mrs. Malloy at the rectory and your own Rory, I'd starve." He glanced toward the doorway, his expression suddenly brightening. "Now, my boy, just look at what the wind's brought in. If this one isn't a sight for sore eyes. Your good deed is already being rewarded."

Ryan's gaze shifted toward the doorway where, indeed, the sight that greeted him was a blessing. A woman that beautiful could improve a man's mood in the blink of an eye. Huge eyes peered around the pub's shadowy interior. Pale, fine skin had been stung pink by the wind. Waves of thick, auburn curls tumbled in disarray to her shoulders. Slender legs, encased in denim and high leather boots, were the inspiration for a man's most erotic fantasies. Ryan sighed with pleasure.

"Boy, where are your manners?" Father Francis scolded. "She's a paying customer who's obviously new to Ryan's Place. Go welcome her."

Casting a sour look at the meddling old man, Ryan crossed to the other end of the crowded bar. "Can I help you, miss?"

"I doubt it," she said grimly. "I doubt all the saints in heaven can solve this one."

Ryan chuckled. "How about a bartender and a cranky old priest? Will we do? Or is there someone you're supposed to be meeting here? I know most of the regulars."

"No, I'm not meeting anyone, but I'd certainly like an introduction to someone who can fix a flat. I've called every garage in a ten-mile radius. Not a one of them has road service tonight. They all point out that tomorrow's Thanksgiving, as if I didn't know that. I have a car loaded with food, thank you very much, and given the way I hate to cook, I flatly refuse to let it all spoil while I'm stuck here. Of course, since the temperature is below freezing, I'm sure I'll have blocks of ice by the time I finally get home."

Ryan wisely bit back another chuckle. "Do you have a spare tire?"

The look she shot him was lethal. "Of course I

have a spare. One of those cute little doughnut things. Don't you think I tried that? I'm not totally helpless."

"Well, then?"

"It's flat, too. What good is the darn thing if it's going to be flat when you need it most?"

Ryan decided not to remind her that it probably needed to be checked once in a while to avoid precisely this kind of situation. She didn't seem to be in the mood for such obviously belated advice.

"How about this?" he suggested. "Have a seat down here by Father Francis. I'll get you something to drink that will warm you up, and we'll discuss the best way to go about solving your problem."

"I don't have time to sit around." She regarded the priest apologetically. "No offense, Father, but I was supposed to be at my parents' house hours ago. I'm sure they're getting frantic."

"Did you—"

She frowned at him and cut him off. "Before you say it, of course I've called. They know what's going on, but you don't know my parents. Until I actually walk in the door, they'll be frantic anyway. It's what they do. They worry. Big things, little things—it doesn't matter. They claim their right to worry about their children came with the birth certificates."

Ryan had a lot of trouble relating to frantic parents. His own hadn't given two hoots about him or his brothers. When he was nine they'd dumped the three oldest boys on the state, then vanished, taking the two-year-old twins with them. If there had been an explanation for their cavalier treatment of their sons, they hadn't bothered to share it with Ryan or his brothers.

He could still remember the last time he'd seen seven-year-old Sean, crying his eyes out as he was led away by a social worker. Michael, two years younger, had been braver by far . . . or perhaps at five he hadn't really understood what was happening to them. They'd never seen each other or their parents again.

Most of the time, Ryan kept those memories securely locked away, but every once in a while they crept out to haunt him . . . most often around holidays. It was yet another reason to despise the occasions when anyone without family felt even more alone than usual.

"You're closing in an hour or so, aren't you, Ryan?" Father Francis asked, snapping him out of his dark thoughts. There was a gleam in the old man's eyes when he added, "Perhaps you could give the young lady a lift home."

Before Ryan could list all the reasons why that was a lousy idea, a pair of sea-green eyes latched on to him. "Could you? I know it's an imposition. I'm sure you have your own Thanksgiving plans, but I truly am desperate."

"What about a cab? I'd be happy to call one, and you'd be home in no time."

"I tried," she said. "It's a long trip, and a lot of the drivers have gone home because of the holiday. There aren't a lot of people out and about. Most are home with their families. Both companies I called turned me down."

"Ryan, my boy, if ever there was a lady in distress, it would seem to be this young woman. Surely you won't be saying no to such a simple thing," Father Francis said.

"I'm a stranger," Ryan pointed out. He scowled at her. "Don't you know you should never accept a ride with a stranger?"

Father Francis chuckled. "I think she can take the word of the priest that you're a positive gentleman. As for the rest, Ryan Devaney, this is . . . ?" He glanced at the young woman and waited.

"Maggie O'Brien," she said.

A beaming smile spread across the priest's face. "Ah, a fine Irish lass, is it? Ryan, you can't possibly think of turning down a fellow countryman."

Ryan suspected Maggie had spent even less time in the Emerald Isle than he had on his ventures to learn the art of running a successful Irish pub. She sounded very much like a Boston native.

"I think we can probably agree that Ms. O'Brien and I are, indeed, fellow Americans," he said wryly.

"But you carry the blood of your Irish ancestors," the priest insisted. "And a true and loyal Irishman never forgets his roots."

"Whatever," Ryan replied, knowing that for the second time tonight he might as well give in to the inevitable. "Ms. O'Brien, I'll be happy to give you a lift if you can wait till I close in an hour. In the meantime I'll give you the keys to my car. You can transfer all that food you're carrying to it." He shot a pointed look at the priest. "Father Francis will be happy to help, won't you, Father?"

"It will be my pleasure," the priest said, bouncing to his feet with more alacrity than he'd shown in the past ten years.

"Ms. O'Brien," Ryan called after them as they headed for the door. "Whatever you do, don't listen to a word he says about me."

"I always sing your praises," Father Francis retorted with a hint of indignation. "By the time I've said my piece, she'll be thinking you were sent here by angels."

"That's exactly what I'm afraid of," Ryan said. For some reason he had a very bad feeling about this Maggie O'Brien getting the idea, even for a second, that he was any sort of saint.

"I'm not sure Mr. Devaney is very happy about doing this," Maggie said to Father Francis as they transferred her belongings from her car to Ryan

Devaney's. She considered leaving the things in the trunk behind, but snow was just starting to fall, the flakes fat and wet. If it kept up as predicted, it was going to make a mess of the roads in no time. There was no telling how long it might be before she'd be able to come back for the car.

"You mustn't mind a thing he says," the priest said. "Ryan's a good lad, but he's been in a bit of a rut. He works much too hard. An unexpected drive with a pretty girl is just what he needs."

It was an interesting spin, Maggie thought, concluding that the priest was doing a bit of matchmaking. She had to wonder, though, why a man like Ryan Devaney would need anyone at all to intercede with women on his behalf. With those clear blue eyes, thick black hair and a dimple in his chin, he had the look of the kind of Irish scoundrel who'd been born to tempt females. Maggie had noticed more than one disappointed look when he'd turned his attention to her at the bar. Come to think of it, quite a few of his customers had been women, in groups and all alone. She wondered how many of them were drawn to the pub by the attractiveness and availability of its owner. Then again, there had been clusters of well-dressed young men around as well, so perhaps *they'd* been the lure for the women.

"Has Ryan's Place been around a long time?" she asked Father Francis.

"It will be nine years come St. Patrick's Day," he told her.

Maggie was surprised. With its worn wood, gleaming brass fixtures and antique advertising signs for Irish whisky and ales, it had the look of a place that had been in business for generations.

The priest grinned at her. "Ah, I see you're surprised. Ryan would be pleased by that. He spent six months in Ireland gathering treasures to give the pub a hint of age. When he makes up his mind to do something, there's nothing halfway about it." He gave her a canny look. "In my opinion, he'll be the same way once he sets his sights on a woman."

Despite the fact that she'd spent less than a half hour with Ryan Devaney, Maggie couldn't deny that she was curious. "He's never been married?"

"No, and it's a sad thing," the priest said. "He says he doesn't believe in love."

He said it with such exaggerated sorrow that Maggie almost laughed. "Now why is that?" she asked instead. "Did he have a relationship that ended badly?"

"Aye, but not like you're thinking. It was his parents. They went off and abandoned him when he was just a wee lad."

"How horrible," Maggie said, instantly sympathetic, which, she suspected, was precisely the reaction the sneaky old man was going for. "He's never been in touch with them again?"

"Never. Despite that and some troubled years, he's grown into a fine man. You won't find a better, more loyal friend than Ryan Devaney."

"How long have you known him?"

"It's been seventeen years now."

Maggie regarded him intently. "Something tells me there's a story there."

"Aye, but I think I'll let Ryan be the one to tell you in his own time." He met her gaze. "Would you mind a bit of advice from a stranger?"

"From you, Father? Of course not."

"Ryan's a bit like a fine wine. He can't be rushed, if you want the best from him."

Maggie laughed. "Father, your advice is a bit premature. I've just met the man. He's giving me a lift home—under pressure from you, I might add. I don't think we can make too much of that."

"Don't be so quick to shatter an old man's dream, or to dismiss the notion of destiny," the priest chided. "Something tells me that destiny has played a hand in tonight's turn of events. You could have had that flat tire anywhere, but where did it happen? Right in front of the finest Irish pub in Boston. Now, let's go back inside, and you can have that drink Ryan promised to warm you up before the drive home."

Maggie followed Father Francis back to the bar. Ryan's hands were full, filling orders for last call, but Irish coffees materialized in front of them without either of them saying a word. Maggie wrapped her icy hands around the cup, grateful for the warmth.

Next to her, Father Francis had fallen silent as he sipped his own coffee. Maggie hadn't been able to guess his age earlier, but now, with his features less animated, the lines in his face were more evident. She guessed him to be well past seventy, and at this late hour he was showing every one of those years.

Apparently, Ryan spotted the same signs of exhaustion, because the apron came off from around his waist and he nabbed one of the waitresses and murmured something to her, then handed her a set of keys.

"We can be going now. Maureen will close up here," he said, stepping out from behind the bar. "Father, I'll give you a ride, as well. It's far too cold a night for you to be walking home, especially at this hour."

"Nonsense. It's only a couple of blocks," the priest protested. "Since when haven't I walked it? Have you once heard me complain? Walking is how I keep myself fit."

"And you do more than enough of it during the day, when the wind's not so fierce. Besides, the rectory is right on our way," Ryan countered, even though he couldn't possibly know in which direction they were heading to get to Maggie's.

She immediately seized on his comment, though, to second the offer. "Father, please. I'd love to catch a glimpse of your church. Maybe I'll come to mass there one of these days."

The priest's expression promptly brightened. "Now, there's a lovely thought. St. Mary's is a wonderful parish. We'd welcome you anytime."

Ryan shot her a grateful look, then led the way outside. If anything, the bite of the wind had grown colder in the last half hour. Maggie shivered, despite the warmth of her coat and scarf. To her surprise, Ryan noticed.

"We'll have you warmed up in no time," he promised. "Once it gets going, the car's heater is like a blast furnace."

The promise was accompanied by a look that could have stirred a teakettle to a boil. For a man who didn't believe in love, he certainly knew how to get a woman's attention. A couple of sizzling glances like that and she'd be begging for air-conditioning.

"I really appreciate this," she told him again. "I know it's an imposition."

"Ryan's happy to do it," Father Francis insisted from the back seat as they pulled to a stop in front of a brownstone town house next to a church. Lights were blazing from the downstairs windows, and smoke curled from a chimney. "I'll say good-night now. It was a pleasure meeting you, Maggie O'Brien. St. Mary's is right next door, as you can see. Don't be a stranger."

"Thanks for all your help, Father."

"What did I do? Nothing that any Irishman wouldn't do for a lady in distress. Happy Thanksgiving, Maggie. Be sure to count your blessings tomorrow. Ryan, you do the same."

"Don't I always, Father?"

"Only when I remind you, which I'm doing now." He paused before closing the door and cast a pointed look in Maggie's direction. "And don't forget to count this one."

Maggie had to bite back a chuckle at Ryan's groan.

"Good night, Father," Ryan said firmly.

He waited as the priest trudged slowly up the steps and went inside, then turned to Maggie. "I'm sorry. My love life has become one of Father Francis's pet projects. He's determined to see me settled with babies underfoot. I apologize if he made you uncomfortable."

"I think it's wonderful that he cares so much," Maggie said honestly. "You're obviously very special to him."

"And vice versa," Ryan admitted.

"He told me you've known each other for a long time," she continued, hoping to open the door to the story that the priest had declined to share.

"A very long time," Ryan confirmed, then looked away to concentrate on roads already slippery from the now-steady snowfall.

Or was he simply avoiding sharing something

painful from his past? Maggie suspected it was the latter, but she recalled the priest's advice about not pushing for answers. Impatient and curious by nature, she found this difficult. It went against everything in her to keep silent, but she managed to bite her tongue.

She turned away and looked out the window just as the car slowed to a stop.

"Maggie?"

She turned and met Ryan's gaze. "Yes?" she said, a little too eagerly. Was it possible that he was going to share the story, after all? Or perhaps suggest another drink before they made the trip to her family's home in neighboring Cambridge?

"It's going to be a long night unless you give me some idea where I'm headed," he said, laughter threading through his voice.

"Oh, my gosh, I am so sorry," she said, feeling foolish. She rattled off the directions to her parents' home, not far from Massachusetts Institute of Technology, where her mother was a professor.

Ryan nodded. "I know the area. I'll have you there in no time. And I can arrange to have your car towed out on Friday, if you like."

Maggie balked at the generous offer. "Absolutely not. It's not your problem. I'll take care of it."

Even as the protest left her mouth, she realized that her stranded car was her only sure link to seeing Ryan Devaney again. She stole a look at him and felt her heart do an unexpected little flip. Such a reaction was not to be ignored. Not that she believed in destiny—at least the way Father Francis interpreted it—but just in case there was such a thing, she didn't want to be too quick to spit in its eye.

Chapter Two

Ryan liked a woman who knew when to keep silent. He truly admired a woman who knew better than to pry. To her credit, Maggie O'Brien was earning a lot of respect on this drive, thanks to her apparent understanding of those two points.

He'd seen the flare of curiosity in her eyes earlier. No telling what Father Francis had seen fit to share with her, but there was little doubt in his mind that the priest had done his level best to whet her interest in Ryan. A lot of women would have seized the opportunity of a long drive on a dark night to pester him with an endless barrage of personal questions, yet Maggie seemed to enjoy the silence as much as he did.

Of course, there could be too much of a good thing, he concluded finally. Any second now he was going to start filling the conversational lull with a litany of questions that had been nagging at him ever since she'd walked into the pub.

Over the years, working at Ryan's Place, he'd managed to put aside his natural reticence in order to make the expected small talk with his customers. Few understood how difficult a task it was for him. In fact, there were those who thought he had a natural gift of the gab and many more who were sure he'd kissed the Blarney Stone during his stay in Ireland.

Outside the pub, though, he tended toward brooding silence. That was probably one reason why the handful of women customers he'd asked out over the years were so surprised to find him less than forthcoming on a date. And since he'd generally asked all the personal questions in which he had an interest during those evenings in the pub, it made him less than scintillating company. Since he had little interest in a long-term relationship, it generally worked out for the best all the way around. Few women pestered him for more than a single date. Those who took his moods as a challenge eventually tired of the game, as well.

Since Maggie O'Brien had never set foot in Ryan's Place before, he had all his usual questions, plus a surprising million and one more personal queries on the tip of his tongue. But because asking them might give her an opening to turn the tables on him, he concluded he'd better keep his curiosity under control.

"Mind if I turn on the radio?" he asked, already reaching for the dial.

She seemed startled that he'd bothered to ask. "Of course not. Whatever you like."

"Any preferences?"

"Jazz," she suggested hesitantly. "Not everyone likes it, I know, but I can't get a single jazz station where I live, and I really miss it."

Ryan was surprised by the choice. "Now, I

would have pegged you as a woman who likes oldies."

"I do, but there's something about a mournful sax that tears my heart up. It's such a melancholy sound." She regarded him worriedly. "If you hate it, though, it's okay. Oldies will be fine."

Ryan flipped on the radio, and sweet jazz immediately filled the car. He grinned at her. "Pre-set to the jazz station," he pointed out. "It seems we have something in common, Maggie O'Brien. Wouldn't that make Father Francis ecstatic?"

"Something tells me we shouldn't offer him any encouragement," she said dryly. "The man does perform weddings, after all. He's liable to have us marching down the aisle before we even know each other."

"Not likely," Ryan murmured, then winced at his own harsh response to what had clearly been nothing more than a teasing remark. "Sorry. Nothing personal."

"No offense taken," Maggie said easily.

But Ryan noticed he'd managed to wipe the smile off her face. Once again she turned away to stare out the window, seemingly fascinated by the falling snow.

And he felt about two inches tall.

Even with the soothing sounds of her favorite jazz to distract her, Maggie couldn't help wondering about the brooding man beside her. Time after time during her brief visit to his pub, she had seen him turn on the charm with his customers. She'd also noted the very real affection between him and the old priest and Ryan's quick recognition of the older man's exhaustion.

Now, however, he'd fallen into a grim silence, apparently content to let the radio fill the silence. She could as easily have been riding with an untalkative cabbie.

When she could stand it no longer, she risked a glance at him. Ever since his offhand comment about the unlikelihood of getting trapped into marrying her by the scheming Father Francis, he'd kept his gaze locked on the road as if it presented some sort of challenge. Since the sky south of town was still clear and bright with stars and there hadn't been a patch of ice on the highway since they'd left downtown Boston, she concluded that he was trying to avoid looking at her. Maybe he feared she shared the priest's determination to create a match between them.

Of course, it was probably for the best. From the moment she'd walked into Ryan's Place and looked into the eyes of the owner, she'd felt a disconcerting twinge of awareness that went way beyond gratitude toward a man who'd offered, albeit reluctantly, to bail her out of a jam. Every time she'd ever gotten a twinge like that, it had landed her in trouble. She had a whole slew of regrets to prove it, though few were romantic in nature. Her impulses tended toward other areas. Some had cost her money. Some had gotten her mixed up in projects that were a waste of her time. Only one had been related to a scoundrel who'd stolen her heart.

Still, she couldn't seem to keep her eyes off him. He was, after all, every girl's fantasy of a Black Irish hunk. She noted again that his coal-black hair, worn just a bit too long, gave him a rakish, bad-boy appearance. His deep blue eyes danced with merriment, at least when he wasn't scowling over having been outmaneuvered by Father Francis, a wily old man if ever she'd met one. There was a tiny scar at the corner of his mouth, barely visible unless one looked closely, which, of course, she had. After all, the man had a mouth that any sane woman would instantly imagine locked against her own.

Yes, indeed, Ryan Devaney was the embodiment of every woman's fantasy, all right. A very dangerous fantasy. It would be all too easy to fall in with Father Francis's scheming.

Ryan Devaney was also a man of contradictions. For one thing, he might have his hard edges and unyielding black moods, but she herself had seen evidence of his tender heart in the way he'd bustled the protesting priest out of the bar and into his car for a ride the few blocks to the rectory. Maggie was a sucker for a man with that particular mysterious combination.

For another thing, Ryan was a successful businessman with the soul of a poet. The rhythm of his words, when he'd lapsed for a moment into an Irish brogue to tease a customer, had been like music to Maggie's ears. She sighed just remembering the lilting sound of his voice. She could still recall sitting on her grandfather O'Brien's knee years ago, enthralled by his tales of the old country, told with just such a musical lilt. Listening to Ryan Devaney, even knowing that the accent was feigned, had taken her back to those happy occasions.

She'd known the man less than two hours, and she was already intrigued in a way that had her heart thumping and her thoughts whirling. She blamed at least some of her reaction on her innate curiosity. Her father was a journalist, always poking his nose into things that he considered the public's business, long before the public even knew they cared. Her mother was a scientist and professor at MIT, a profession that managed to combine her curiosity about how the universe worked and her nurturing skills.

Inevitably, living with two people like that, Maggie had grown up with an insatiable desire to understand what made people tick. She had a trace of her father's cynicism, a healthy dose of her mother's reason and an intuitive ability to see beneath the surface.

Among her friends she was the one they turned

to when they were trying to make sense of relationships, when a boss was giving them trouble, when a parent was making impossible demands. Maggie always had a helpful insight, if not a solution, to offer.

The only life she couldn't seem to make sense of was her own. She was still struggling to carve out a niche for herself. She had a degree in business and in accounting, but in one of those contradictions that she seemed to like in others, she kept searching for a creative outlet that would feed her soul as well as her bank account.

Her last job certainly hadn't offered that. She'd loved the small coastal town in Maine, which was why she'd persuaded herself that she could be happy doing bookkeeping for a small corporation. In the end, though, the early-morning strolls on the beach, the quaint shops and the friendly neighbors hadn't compensated for the daily tedium in her job. She'd given her notice two weeks ago, on the same day she'd broken off a relationship that had been going nowhere.

Now she was the one in need of direction, but she'd given herself until after the start of the new year to figure things out. With savings in the bank, she didn't have to rush right into another job. She was going to stay with her parents, brothers and sisters for the next few weeks, then decide if she wanted to return to Maine, where she'd been making her home for the past four years, and look for more satisfying work and a relationship that had more excitement and more promise of a future.

With all that heavy thinking awaiting her, Ryan Devaney and his contradictions offered a tempting distraction. She glanced his way again, noting that his focus on the road was no less intense.

"I'm sorry to disrupt your plans this way," she apologized yet again, hoping to spark a conversation.

"Not a problem," he said without looking at her.

"Most people have a lot to do around the holidays."

"It's okay," he said, his delectable mouth drawing into a tight line.

"Will the pub be open tomorrow?"

"For a few hours. Some of our customers have nowhere else to spend Thanksgiving."

She recalled what Father Francis had said about Ryan having been abandoned by his parents. Obviously, he could relate to customers who were essentially in the same fix—all alone in the world. "It's thoughtful of you to give them a place where they'll feel welcome."

"It's a business decision," he said, dismissing the idea that there was any sentiment involved.

"Your own family doesn't mind?" she asked, deliberately feigning ignorance and broaching the touchy subject in the hope that he would open up and fill in the blanks left by Father Francis's sketchy explanation.

"No," he said tightly.

"Tell me about them," she prodded.

He glanced at her then. "There's nothing to tell."

There was a bleak note in his voice she doubted he realized was there. "Oh?" she said. "Every family has a story."

His frown deepened. "Ms. O'Brien, I offered you a lift home. I didn't offer to provide the entertainment. If you need some noise, turn up the radio."

Maggie hesitated at the sharp tone, but even an armchair psychologist understood that defensiveness was often a cover for a deep-seated need to talk. She wondered if Ryan Devaney had ever talked about whatever he was trying so determinedly to keep from her. Maybe he told his secrets to Father Francis from the shadows of the confessional, or maybe the priest was simply better at prying them loose.

"Sometimes it's easier to tell things to a stranger than it is to a friend," she observed lightly.

"And sometimes there's nothing to tell," he repeated.

Though she already knew at least some of the answers, she decided to try getting them directly from the source. "Are you married?" she began.

"No."

"Have you ever been?"

"No."

"What about the rest of your family?"

He slammed on the brakes and turned to glower at her. "I have no family," he said tightly. "None at all. Are you satisfied, Ms. O'Brien?"

Satisfied? Far from it, she thought as she gazed into eyes burning with anger. If anything, she was more intrigued than ever. Now, however, was probably not the best time to tell Ryan that. Maybe tomorrow, after she'd persuaded him to stay and spend Thanksgiving with her family, maybe then he'd be mellow enough to explain what had happened years ago to tear his world apart and why he claimed to have no family at all, when the truth was slightly different. They might not be in his life, but they were more than likely out there somewhere.

Even without all the answers, Maggie was filled with sympathy. Because with two parents, three sisters and two brothers, a couple of dozen aunts, uncles and cousins—all of them boisterous, impossible, difficult and undeniably wonderful—she couldn't imagine anyone having no one at all to call family.

Ryan caught the little flicker of dismay in Maggie's eyes when he'd announced that he had no family to speak of. He was pretty sure he'd seen something else, as well, a faint glint of determination.

Maybe that was why he wasn't the least bit surprised when she invited him to stay over once they reached her family's large house off Kendall Square.

"It's nearly two in the morning," she told him. "You must be exhausted. Please stay. I'm sure there's an overflow crowd here tonight, but there's bound to be a couch or something free. If worse comes to worst, I know there are sleeping bags in the attic. I can set you up with one of those."

"Don't worry about it. I'm used to late nights. I'll be fine," he insisted as he began unloading bags from his trunk. Since she and Father Francis had loaded the car, it was the first time he'd realized that she must have half her worldly possessions with her. He regarded her wryly. "You planning on a long visit?"

"Till after New Year's," she said.

"What about your job? You do have one, I imagine."

"I'm between jobs," she said.

"Fired?" he asked, pulling out the familiar note of sympathy he used when his customers hit a similar rough patch.

"Nope. I quit a very good job as an accountant for a corporation. I'm hoping to find something that's more creatively satisfying."

"Such as?"

She shrugged. "I wish I knew," she said, then added with a note of total optimism, "but I'll figure it out."

"Ever considered psychology?" Ryan asked. "You've got the probing-question thing down pretty well."

"I can't be too good," she retorted. "You didn't answer most of them."

"So what sort of career do you think you'd find creatively satisfying?" he continued. "Are there any options on the table?"

She grinned. "Trying to turn things around on me, Mr. Devaney?"

He laughed. "Every bartender has a bit of the psychologist in him. The difference is, we just ask questions and listen. We don't dole out advice. Now let's get this stuff inside before we both freeze to death."

"We'll go around back," she said, leading the way. "A lot of this needs to wind up in the kitchen, anyway."

He noted that there was a light on in one of the front windows, as well as another in the kitchen, beaming out a welcome for the latecomer. A little tug of envy spread through him even before a tall woman with a face only barely more lined than Maggie's threw open the kitchen door and held out her arms.

"There you are," she said, enveloping Maggie in a fierce hug. "I've been so worried."

"Mom, I called less than forty minutes ago to let you know I was on my way," Maggie reminded her, amusement threading through her voice. "I'm actually about ten minutes earlier than I predicted."

"Which means you must have been speeding, young man," the woman chastised, turning to Ryan with a twinkle in eyes as bright and as green as her daughter's. "I'm Nell O'Brien. And you must be Mr. Devaney. It was kind of you to bring Maggie to us, even if you did exceed the speed limit getting her here."

"No, ma'am, I can assure you there was no speeding involved," he responded seriously. "I had it on cruise control the whole time."

She laughed at that. "But set at what speed?"

Ryan met her gaze. "You're not a cop, are you?" he teased, liking her at once. She reminded him of . . . He bit back a sigh. Best not to go there. He'd stopped thinking about his mother on the day she'd abandoned him. Or at least he'd tried to.

"No, but I've had a lot of experience at intimidating young men," Mrs. O'Brien said. "I have four daughters and two sons, all of whom need to have someone in firm control."

Ryan couldn't help the grin that spread across his face. "If Maggie here is any indication, I imagine that's true."

"Hey," Maggie protested. "I was the dutiful oldest daughter."

"When it suited you," her mother concurred. "Now get in here, both of you. I have coffee made, but if you'd prefer something else, I can fix it in no time."

"Nothing for me," Ryan said, already backing toward the door. The warmth of this big, cheerful kitchen, the teasing between mother and daughter—these were exactly the kind of things he tried to avoid. They brought up too many painful memories. "I need to be getting back home."

"Absolutely not," Mrs. O'Brien said. "It's much too late to be on the road, Mr. Devaney. You must be exhausted. I'll make up the couch in the den. And before you try arguing with me, remember that I'm older and wiser and I will not be ignored."

"If you're not a cop, you must be a general," Ryan said.

"Just a woman who knows what's best," Nell countered with a serene smile. "You two stay in here and have something to drink and a snack. I'll go on up to bed after I'm done in the den. Your father will want to know you arrived safely, Maggie. Besides, I have to be up at dawn to cook that bird." She winked at Maggie. "Your father bought a huge one that's probably not going to fit in the oven, which means I'll have to surgically dissect the thing, then patch it back together after it's cooked so he won't know."

Ryan saw his chance for escape coming right after Mrs. O'Brien disappeared for the night, but one look at Maggie had him hesitating.

"Don't even think about," she said, her gaze locked with his.

"Think about what?" he asked vaguely, his thoughts scrambling.

"Sneaking away in the dead of night."

"Any particular reason?"

"Because tomorrow's going to be a busy day as it is. I don't want to have to spend a chunk of it hunting you down and dragging you back here."

"So this is purely selfish on your part," he said, taking a step closer to the dangerous fire in her eyes. There was something about her—an exuberance, a warmth—that made him want to take risks he normally avoided.

"It is," she said, her gaze unflinching.

"Maggie, I did you a small favor. You don't owe me anything. Besides, I have plans for tomorrow, and the day starts early. I really do need to be getting back."

Surprise flickered in her eyes then. "You have plans?"

He was vaguely insulted by her obvious shock. "I'm not totally hopeless and alone."

She blinked and backed up a step. "Yes, of course. I should have realized," she said, clearly embarrassed.

Ryan should have let her go on thinking that

those plans involved another woman, which was clearly the conclusion she'd reached. That would have been the smart, safe way to go. Instead, he found himself explaining.

"I'm taking food to the homeless shelter run by St. Mary's. Everything has to be set up by noon, which means an early start. And, as we discussed in the car, the pub opens at four for the regulars who don't have anyplace else to go. Not to mention that tonight's paperwork didn't get done, nor were the receipts counted."

She nodded and something that might have been relief flashed across her face. "What a wonderful thing to do," she said, apparently seizing on the planned meal for the homeless. "Can you use some help at the shelter?"

Help was always in short supply, but Ryan hesitated. It would be better to stop things here and now with this woman who had the determination of a pit bull and who seemed eager and able to slip past all his defenses.

"Of course you can," she said, without waiting for his reply. "We'll be at the shelter by ten."

" 'We'?"

"My family, except for Mom, of course. She'll need to stay here with that humongous bird, but everyone else will want to pitch in. It works out perfectly. I'll have one of my brothers bring along a spare for my car, too."

Ryan searched desperately for a subtle way to

change her mind. "Shouldn't your family be pitching in around here?"

"Mom refuses to let anyone else into the kitchen. She says we just get in the way. Besides, I brought a lot of food tonight that only needs to go in the oven. Everyone else will bring dishes, too. She really has only the turkey to contend with." Maggie regarded him intently. "Don't even think of turning me down. I owe you."

"You don't," he repeated, even though he knew he was wasting his breath.

Besides, one part of him—a very big part—was suddenly looking forward to Thanksgiving in a way that he hadn't since he was eight years old. That was the last holiday his family had spent together. By Christmas that year, he'd been with a foster family, and he'd had no idea at all where his parents or his brothers were.

And nothing in his life had been the same since.

Chapter Three

"Late night last night?" Rory inquired as he and Ryan loaded food into a van to take it to the homeless shelter. "You look a wee bit under the weather."

Ryan scowled at his cook's apparent amusement. "I did a favor for Father Francis. It kept me out until after 3:00 a.m."

"And did this favor happen to involve a lovely redheaded lass?"

Ryan gave him a sour look.

"I thought so. Why is it that Father Francis never thinks of me when a beauty like that comes along?" Rory lamented.

"Perhaps because he's well aware of your tendency to break the heart of any woman you go out with," Ryan told him. "You've earned a bit of a reputation in your time among us, Rory, me lad."

"Undeserved, every word of it," Rory insisted.

"Then why do I have a steady stream of women at the bar crying into their beers over you?"

"I can't help it if I'm a babe magnet," the cook said with a perfectly straight face.

The irony was that despite his round shape and fiery temperament, forty-year-old Rory attracted more than his share of women. Ryan suspected it had something to do with his clever way with words and his genuine appreciation of the fair sex. Rory's problem was that he appreciated a few too many females at one time. The drama of the breakups frequently spilled from the kitchen into the pub. Oddly enough, even after the blowups, the women kept coming around. Rory treated each and every one of them with the same cheerful affection.

"I can hardly wait for you to fall head-over-heels in love," Ryan told him. "I truly hope the woman makes you jump through hoops, so I can sit on the sidelines and enjoy the entertainment."

"I feel the same where you're concerned," Rory responded. He regarded Ryan with a speculative look. "So, has this redheaded angel of Father Francis's well and truly caught your eye? Or am I free to pursue her next time she stops in?"

"Stay away from Maggie," Ryan retorted, unable to keep a fiercely possessive note out of his voice. He swore to himself that he was only thinking of Maggie's heart, not his own.

Rory grinned. "So, that's the way of it? Father Francis will be pleased to know that his clever machinations have worked at last. Can it be that our Ryan has finally found a woman who can hold his interest beyond a one-night stand?"

Ryan scowled at him. "Don't be ridiculous. I barely know the woman."

"Has there ever been an Irishman born who doesn't believe that a lightning bolt can strike at any time? Love doesn't always require years of nurturing to blossom, you know."

"Thanks for the unsolicited lesson," Ryan said dryly.

"I have much more wisdom I could impart," Rory claimed cheerfully. "But why should I waste it on a man who's determined to go through life alone?"

"You know, if you don't learn to watch your tongue, I could fire you."

"But you won't," Rory said confidently. "Who would cook your authentic Irish cuisine?"

"Maybe I'll change the menu," Ryan said, thinking of the newest addition to his staff.

"Not bloody likely," Rory said.

"I don't know. I've got someone coming by tomorrow. Father Francis thinks she'll do rather well."

Rory frowned. "Another cook?"

"Yes."

"And would this be the angelic Maggie, by any chance?" Rory inquired hopefully.

"Absolutely not."

"Is she from Ireland, at least?"

"No."

"Well, there you go. How good can she be?"

"I've heard only raves," Ryan said honestly. "She's supposed to be excellent, so of course I hired her sight unseen."

"She's not coming for an interview? You've

already hired a woman you've never even met for my kitchen?" Rory demanded, clearly horrified. "I can't have some stranger—and a woman at that—underfoot all day."

"Why not? Will she be a distraction? Surely you can rise above your need to make a play for anything wearing skirts, especially since this one's married. And just in case you're tempted, you should know that her husband will be working in front." He gave Rory a steady look. "I don't think it will be a problem, do you? There are some lines not even you will cross."

Rory groaned. "These are more of Father Francis's strays, aren't they? I suppose we will find them at the shelter today, am I right?"

Ryan saw little point in denying it. He nodded. He considered telling Rory the rest, that his new helper barely spoke English and prepared only Mexican dishes, but decided his friend had had enough of a shock for the moment. Instead, he simply reminded him that there was a replacement waiting in the wings. "So, let that be a warning to keep a civil tongue in your head. And when you meet her today, be nice."

"When am I not kind to everyone who works at the pub?" Rory demanded indignantly.

Ryan rolled his eyes. "You don't want me to answer that, do you?"

"Okay, okay, I'll be nice." He regarded Ryan

curiously. "Are you going to be seeing Maggie again?"

"She says she's going to bring her family to help out at the shelter today," he admitted rue-fully.

"Well now, isn't that splendid? Father Francis will have yet another blessing to count on Thanksgiving."

"Go to hell, Rory."

To Ryan's disgust, the big man merely laughed. As far as Ryan could see, this was not a laughing matter. He was apparently surrounded by match-makers who were going to take a great deal of delight in seeing him squirm. And they'd both handpicked Maggie for the task of accomplishing it, quite possibly because they'd both seen what he hadn't been willing to admit—that he was attracted to her.

The noise level in the O'Brien dining room was at an all-time high, with squealing toddlers scrambling for Maggie's attention and her brothers fighting for the biggest share of her mother's pancakes. It was all music to her ears, even if she couldn't seem to get a word in edge-wise.

When her third attempt to interrupt the nonstop bickering fell on deaf ears, Maggie sent a beseeching look toward her mother.

"Enough!" Nell O'Brien said without even

raising her voice to be heard above the din. It was her quiet, emphatic tone that caused even the littlest grandchild to fall silent. The skill had to be something she'd acquired in the classroom to control unruly college students. Clearly satisfied by the effect, she said mildly, "I think Maggie has something she'd like to say."

"Since when does Maggie require your intervention?" Matthew asked. "Speak up, sis. You've never been shy about telling us to shut up before."

"You've never been this noisy before, and I'm out of practice," she retorted. "Okay, here's the deal. I more or less promised that we'd spend this morning helping at a homeless shelter in the city."

"Promised who?" Matthew demanded with more curiosity than resentment.

"Must be that handsome man who brought her home last night," her sister Colleen said with a smug expression. "Mom says after meeting him last night, her heart was still all aflutter this morning. I'm sorry I missed him. Count me in, Maggie. I want to get a look at any guy who can make Mom swoon."

"There's definitely a man involved?" their oldest brother, John, asked. "Then we all go, am I right? We can't have a stranger breaking our Maggie's heart."

"This has nothing to do with anyone breaking

my heart," Maggie said. "It's about helping those less fortunate on Thanksgiving."

"That may be *your* reason for going," John conceded. "Mine's less pure."

"Mine, too," Colleen said. "My heart hasn't gone pitter-pat over a man in ages."

"Thanks a lot," her husband said, frowning at her.

Colleen grinned at him. "I meant for a man other than *you,* of course."

Daniel leaned over and planted a noisy kiss on her lips. "That's better, love."

"What's this about a handsome man?" Katie, the youngest O'Brien, inquired as she returned from the kitchen with a glass of orange juice. "Where? Can I meet him?"

"He's entirely too old for you," Maggie said.

"That's the truth," her father chimed in. "Our Katie's not to even think of looking at a man until she's at least twenty-five. She's our baby."

Katie rolled her eyes. "Dad, I'm twenty-four, and I hate to break it to you, but I'm already dating and have been for some years now."

"Dating, yes, but you've a full year to go before you even think of getting serious about anyone. Besides, this Ryan fellow is Maggie's," he said with a grin aimed at Maggie.

"He's hardly that," Maggie protested. "We've just met."

"But you're interested enough to be dragging us

all the way to Boston on Thanksgiving," her father said. He turned to her mother. "Nell, what do you think? Is this man worthy of our Maggie's attention?"

With a wink in Maggie's direction, her mother placed her hand over her heart. "If I were just a few years younger . . ." she began, only to be cut off by her husband.

"Nell O'Brien, shame on you, saying such a thing in front of me, the man who's given you all these fine children, to say nothing of nearly thirty years of my life."

"Darling, I'm old and I'm married, not dead," she teased. "Ryan Devaney is a handsome devil. You'll see."

"So it's settled? You'll all go?" Maggie asked, not as concerned about her brothers' declared motives as she probably should have been. They talked big, but they'd stay in line. Her father would see to it.

"Of course," her father said. "You knew we would." He turned to his wife. "You'll be okay without our help for a few hours?"

"I'll be relieved to have you all out from underfoot," she said.

"What about the kids? You can't be looking after all of them, as well," her father said. He gazed around the crowded table. "Which one of you will stay to help out?"

"Garrett O'Brien, the day I can't look after

three toddlers is the day they'll be putting me in my grave," her mother retorted. "I raised this bunch of hellions with little or no help, didn't I?"

"Then it's settled," her father announced. "We'll be leaving in an hour. That will put us there by ten. Is that what you promised, Maggie?"

"Yes, Dad. Thanks." She turned a narrowed gaze on her brothers. "And when you meet Ryan Devaney, I expect you to be on your best behavior. Is that understood?"

"When have we not been perfect gentlemen around your boyfriends?" Matt inquired indignantly.

"Well, there was the time we ran off that Carson fellow," John conceded.

"He was a wuss," Matt countered. "She was better off without him. Okay, aside from that one incident, have there been any others?"

"Just see that this isn't one of those times when your protective instincts kick into gear," Maggie pleaded. She shot a warning look at Katie. "And you remember what Dad said."

A grin spread across her sister's face. "You are staking your claim, then?" She turned to their father. "Told you I could make her admit it. That'll be five bucks, please."

Maggie stared at the two of them. "You already knew about Ryan and you had a bet going?"

"Well, of course we did," Katie said. "It's taken

you practically forever to show an interest in anyone."

"I'm picky."

"You're impossible."

"I was beginning to worry that I'd have to explain to my children about their poor old aunt Maggie living all alone up in Maine in a cold and lonely spinster's cottage."

"I ought to make you stay home today," Maggie declared.

"As if you could," Katie responded. "Watching you get all starry-eyed over some man is going to be better than watching you stuffing tissues in the bodice of your prom dress."

"Katie O'Brien, that was supposed to be our secret forever," Maggie said, as everyone at the table hooted.

"Which just goes to prove you should never trust a kid sister," Katie retorted.

"I'll remember that. Just wait till you bring home the man of your dreams," Maggie said direly.

"Now, girls, that's enough squabbling," their father said, ever the peacemaker. "Today's a day to be grateful for family."

"And I am," Maggie said. "At least all family except my traitorous baby sister."

Now not only did she have to worry about Ryan's reaction to her arrival at the shelter, but which one of her family members was likely to be first to try to embarrass her.

• • •

The St. Mary's Shelter was just down the block from the church. When Maggie and her family arrived, it was already bustling with activity. Even so, Father Francis spotted her the minute she walked in and came over with a welcoming smile.

"Ryan mentioned you might be here this morning. Thank you for spending part of your holiday with us. It's a generous thing you're doing." He surveyed the group with her and beamed. "And this must be your family."

Maggie introduced the priest to everyone, even as her gaze searched the room for some sign of Ryan. Father Francis caught her.

"You'll find Ryan and Rory in the kitchen," he told her with a grin. "But if I were you I'd stay out from underfoot for now. Our Rory is a bit of a tyrant. He has them on a tight time schedule. He'll not be wanting any distractions. I believe the ladies can use some help with setting the tables." He turned to her father and brothers. "And your help will be welcome in setting up the remaining tables and chairs. We're expecting a large crowd today, so we'll have to keep things moving. The first guests will arrive at noon and the last won't be out of here much before three."

Maggie, Colleen and Katie went to work with the other women, though Maggie was constantly on the lookout for Ryan.

"Where is he?" Katie demanded when there had been not so much as a glimpse of him for more than an hour.

"You heard Father Francis," Maggie said. "He's helping in the kitchen. And where is Colleen, by the way?"

"I haven't seen her for some time now," Katie said. "*She's* probably in the kitchen where you should be. Can't you think of some excuse to go in there? If you don't, I will."

"Katie O'Brien, you'll do no such thing," Maggie protested. "We came here to help where we're needed, not to gawk at Ryan Devaney."

Katie grinned. "Then you're no sister of mine. I'd rather look at a handsome man any day than make sure the place settings are lined up properly."

"He'll come out of the kitchen eventually," Maggie said. "Until then I'm not bothering him."

"Patience won't earn you sainthood," Katie admonished. "And I'm not sure it's ever done much to snag a man."

"I am not out to snag Ryan," Maggie insisted. "I'm just a little curious about him."

Colleen arrived just in time to overhear her remark. "We're all spending part of our holiday at a homeless shelter just so you can satisfy your curiosity?" she asked skeptically. "I don't think so. We're here because you have the hots for this guy. And since I just came from the kitchen where I got a good look at him, I have to say, way to go, Maggie!"

"You've been in the kitchen?" Katie demanded, looking as if she'd been cheated out of her favorite dessert. "Then I'm going."

Maggie scowled at both of them. "Don't make me regret asking you to come today."

"I just want to see what he looks like," Katie argued. "Where's the harm in that? I'm sure Colleen didn't go in there and create a scene."

Just then the kitchen door swung open and Ryan emerged, bearing a huge platter of sliced turkey and followed by a large man carrying trays filled with sweet potatoes and dressing. Ryan's hair was tousled, his blue shirt perfectly matched his eyes, and he was wearing snug jeans that hugged his narrow hips. Maggie's mouth went dry, putting to rest any notion that she was here merely to satisfy her curiosity.

"Oh, my," Katie murmured, then gazed at Maggie with approval. "Your taste has definitely improved while you've been away. Not a one of the men you've dragged home in the past held a candle to *this* one."

Before Maggie could respond, Ryan caught sight of her. A slow smile spread across his face, but then his gaze shifted to the commotion at the shelter door, where a long line of people waited impatiently to be admitted. His expression grew troubled, and he turned to murmur a few words to the man next to him, who surveyed the long line, then nodded and hurried back to the kitchen.

Ryan walked in Maggie's direction. Hoping to stave off an embarrassing interrogation, she escaped her sisters and went to meet him.

"I see you're here to do your good deed," he said.

Maggie ignored the faint edge in his voice. "I promised I would be," she said cheerfully.

His gaze clashed with hers. "Not everyone keeps their word."

"*I* do," she said emphatically, returning his gaze with an unflinching look. "I saw you looking at the crowd a minute ago. Is there a problem?"

"The line is longer than I anticipated. I was just asking Rory if he thought we had enough food. He's convinced we do, but he's gone back to the pub to bring over another turkey just in case."

"Is there anything I can do? There are some stores open today. I could make a run to pick up extra food."

"No need. I'm sure Rory has it under control. What about your family, Maggie? Did you convince them to come today?"

"My sisters are over there," she said, noting that Colleen and Katie were staring at them with unabashed curiosity.

Ryan grinned. "Ah, yes, I recognize one of them. She was in the kitchen earlier. I thought she seemed a bit more interested in me than in the whereabouts of the napkins she claimed to be looking for."

"Sorry about that. Nosiness is a family trait, I'm afraid."

"And your brothers? Are they around?"

"Along with my father," she told him. "They're scattered here and there. Father Francis has seen to it that none of us are idle."

A genuine, full-wattage smile spread across his face then. "Watch out for Father Francis," he warned. "He'll have you all signed up for regular duty here before the day's out, if you're not careful. When it comes to caring for his strays, he's totally shameless."

"I can think of worse places to spend my time," Maggie said.

Her answer seemed to disconcert him for some reason. He promptly mumbled an excuse and headed back to the kitchen, leaving her to stare after him.

For the rest of the afternoon, she caught only glimpses of him as he worked. He seemed to know most of the people there. He joked with the men, flirted with the women and teased the children, but there was always a hint of reserve just below the surface. Whenever he happened to catch Maggie watching him, he quickly looked away as if he feared that she might see beneath the superficial charm.

Even her brothers, usually oblivious to such things, noticed the byplay between them.

"Sis, he's all wrong for you," her younger brother warned. "Too many secrets. And don't even think about making him one of your projects. I don't think he'll appreciate it. Something tells me your Ryan is troubled by dark moods."

"When has that ever stopped me?" she replied.

"Unfortunately, never," Matt said. "But this time you could be in way over your head."

"Have you even talked to him?" she asked testily.

"You wanted us to steer clear of him," John reminded her.

"As if my wishes ever mattered to you before," she scoffed. "Well, if you had talked to Ryan, you would see that he's one of the good guys. In fact, you ought to know that just from the fact that he's here today."

She glanced across the room to where Ryan was serving slices of pumpkin pie to a very pregnant woman and her two dark-haired children. The look on his face was impossible to interpret, but she tried nonetheless. Dismay and sorrow seemed to mingle with friendly concern. She had the sense that he was talking to this woman but seeing something else entirely, something from his own past, perhaps.

Drawn by the scene, she found an excuse to

head for the kitchen, slipping in long enough to grab several pies. When she emerged, she was close enough to hear Ryan murmuring encouraging words to the woman. He seemed to be holding out the promise of a job to help her family get back on its feet. A few minutes later he slipped the husband some money and told him to make sure his wife saw a doctor.

"Come to the pub tomorrow," he told the man. "We'll work out your hours then."

The man beamed at him. "*Gracias, señor.* Thank you. Rosita and I will be there. We are very hard workers. You'll see. You will never have reason to regret giving us this chance."

Ryan sighed as the man went to join his wife. Maggie stepped up behind him.

"That was very nice, what you did just then," she said.

Ryan whirled around, almost dropping the plate he was holding. "Where did you come from?"

"I've been here for hours."

He gave her a sour look. "Believe me, I'm well aware of that. I've had to field more than one question about the red-haired angel with the ready smile. You've drawn more attention around here today than the turkey." He didn't sound especially pleased about it. "I was referring to your popping up just now. Were you eavesdropping on a private conversation?"

"Nope, just bringing out more pies," she said, holding up the armload she'd retrieved from the kitchen. "I couldn't help overhearing what you were saying. You're hiring them?"

He shrugged as if it were nothing. "They need work. I can take on a couple of extra people at this time of year. It's no big deal."

"I'm sure it is to them." Then, to avoid prolonging a topic that obviously made him uncomfortable, she asked, "I understand you're responsible for providing all this food every year. It's very generous of you."

"I have a restaurant. Rory likes to cook for people who appreciate a fine meal," he said. "Why not help out a good cause?"

Once again he'd dismissed his good deed. She probably should have been impressed by his humility, but she found it oddly worrisome, instead. "Why aren't you comfortable accepting a compliment?" she asked.

"Maybe it's because I don't deserve it," he said. "I wasn't the one basting turkeys and pouring pumpkin custard into pie shells all night long. Rory did that, as he has ever since he came to work for me."

"But I imagine you paid for the ingredients and for Rory's time," she countered.

"For the ingredients, yes, but not for Rory's time. He knows, as I do, what it's like to do without on a holiday. We try to make sure that at least some people don't have to know that feeling."

She studied him intently. "How long have you been doing this?"

"Not that it matters, but ever since I opened the pub. And that's enough of that," he said, closing the door on the topic. "I'm sure Father Francis is grateful to you and your family for coming to help out today."

"It's been . . ." She searched for the right word. While helping out had been rewarding, it was what she'd discovered about Ryan Devaney that had been truly important to her. "It's been enlightening."

His gaze narrowed at her comment. "I'm glad we've been able to provide a bit of entertainment for your holiday," he said with a touch of bitterness. "Excuse me. I have things to do."

He brushed past her, but Maggie reached for his arm. When she touched him, she felt the muscle jerk beneath her fingers. Only when he turned to face her did she speak. "You know that I did not mean that to be insulting," she said quietly. "Who did this to you? Who made you distrust everyone the way you do?"

Ryan hesitated, his expression still angry. "It's a long story, and today's not the time," he said finally, his voice tight.

Maggie's gaze was unrelenting. "Will there be a time?"

His gaze locked with hers, and for the longest time she thought he was going to say no, but eventually he sighed heavily.

"I imagine you'll insist on it," he said.

Maggie laughed at the note of resignation in his voice. It wasn't a very big opening, but it was enough. "Yes, Ryan Devaney, you can count on it."

Because despite all the roadblocks he'd set up and all the alarms going off in her head warning her away, she was very much intrigued with everything about this man.

Chapter Four

Ryan was still reeling from the fact that Rosita Gomez, the cook who barely spoke English and knew nothing about Irish food, also happened to be seven months' pregnant. Father Francis had delicately neglected to mention that fact to Ryan when he'd been touting her for a job at the pub. Ryan could hardly wait to see Rory's face when he found out. Thankfully, he'd been able to keep the two of them apart at the shelter yesterday. Rory had been too busy to spend much time in the dining room.

But it wouldn't be long now. Rosita and her husband were due at the pub at two to fill out the necessary paperwork. When Ryan heard the tap on his office door, he assumed it was his two new employees. Instead, he found himself staring at Maggie O'Brien. A sigh escaped before he could stop it.

"You again," he murmured.

"I hope this isn't a bad time," she said.

Ryan desperately wanted to think of an excuse to run her off, but none occurred to him.

"No, it's fine," he said, trying to hide his reluctance. "I have a few minutes before my next appointment. Come on in. What brings you into Boston today?"

She held up an armload of shopping bags. "The

sales," she said. "Surely you know this is one of the biggest shopping days of the year. Black Friday, when businesses expect to go from red ink to black for the year."

"I believe I have read that somewhere," Ryan said dryly. "An ad or two, maybe? Every TV newscast since last week?"

She laughed. "Probably so."

"That still doesn't explain why you're here. Don't tell me you happened to have another flat outside my pub because your car's overloaded."

"Nope. I have four brand-new tires, thanks to my brother. Matt took the car in this morning, muttering the whole time about how irresponsible I was to let the tires get into such sorry shape in the first place. It made him feel very male and very superior, so I suppose there was a blessing to be had."

"Well—" Ryan began.

"Don't you start. Not when I've come bearing gifts."

Ryan's gaze narrowed. "Gifts?"

She frowned at him. "Not for you. While my sisters and I were at the sales, we saw a few things we thought Rosita might be able to use for herself and the baby. That is who you're expecting this afternoon, right? I spoke to her briefly after you and I talked yesterday. I know she wasn't able to bring much with her to the shelter. Wait till you see." She poked around in the shopping bags and started pulling out baby clothes, an expression of pure delight on her face. "Aren't these the cutest things you've ever seen? Look at this." She held up a tiny little knit cap in pale yellow. "And this." She retrieved an outfit with ducks embroidered across the front.

When she had his entire desk covered with baby clothes, she sat back. "What do you think?"

"I think you're amazing," Ryan blurted, then regretted it when he saw the smile that spread across her face. "I meant that Rosita is going to be amazed. Why did you do it? You must have spent a fortune."

"Everything was on sale," she reminded him. "And we couldn't resist." She held up another huge bag. "There are a few maternity outfits in here for Rosita. These are new, but I have another bag in the car of Colleen's old maternity clothes. She swears she will never need them again, but if you ask me Daniel will talk her into at least two more kids. He wants a huge family. He was an only child."

Ryan's head was spinning. "Colleen is the sister who was ogling me in the kitchen?"

Maggie nodded.

"And Daniel is . . . ?"

"Her husband."

"Was he at the shelter yesterday?"

"He was there, along with my father and both of my brothers, plus my youngest sister, Katie. My other sister lives too far away to get home for Thanksgiving, but they'll be here for Christmas. You can't imagine the chaos."

Oddly enough, he could. After the twins were born, there had been five children in the Devaney house for two Christmases. Somehow his parents had always seen to it that there were gifts under the tree, even if they were secondhand toys from the thrift shop in the neighborhood. From the moment he and his brothers had crept downstairs to see if Santa had come, the house had been filled with noise and laughter.

At least that's the way it had been for a few brief years. Then they'd all been separated, and after that, Christmas had been one more day to be endured, worse than all the other days, because he'd wondered where his brothers were and if they were happier than he was. As he'd drifted from foster home to foster home, always feeling like an outsider, he'd prayed they were.

"Ryan?" Maggie asked softly, her gaze filled with concern. "Is something wrong?"

"No," he said tightly. "Everything's fine. Why don't you stick around and give these things to Rosita? She should be here any minute."

Maggie shook her head. "I don't want to embarrass her."

"She'll want to thank you, I'm sure."

"Another time. I should go before she gets here," she insisted, already heading for the door.

"Wait. Didn't you say something about having some clothes for Rosita in the car? I'll walk you out," Ryan said, surprised that he wasn't quite ready to see the last of her. She was pushy and intrusive. In fact, she promised to make a nuisance of herself. But she was also warm and generous, a real ray of sunshine. Like a cat seeking warmth on a windowsill he felt himself drawn to her, despite all of his deep-seated reservations about getting involved with anyone.

As he watched her walk to her car, he realized that one of these days he was going to have to decide which mattered more—protecting himself from her prying or accepting her into his heart.

"You weren't in there long," Colleen commented, after Maggie had retrieved the bag of used maternity clothes, given them to Ryan and said goodbye. She had noticed that he'd kept a careful distance between himself and the car once he'd realized that her sister was waiting for her.

"Long enough," Maggie said, satisfied with herself. The meeting had gone precisely the way she'd hoped it would. She had stayed just long enough to remind Ryan that she intended to be a part of his life—at least for the immediate future—but had left before he'd grown weary of her. And with his reluctance so apparent, she hadn't pressed him to say hello to Colleen. Contact with her family seemed to disturb him, either because he was fearful of getting too involved or because seeing them brought back too many painful memories of the family he'd lost.

"What did he think of all the baby things?" Colleen asked.

"I think he was dumbfounded."

"Clever of you to find a way to plant the notion of babies in his head. Now he won't be able to look at you without thinking about having a baby of his own."

"Colleen, that is *not* what this was about," Maggie protested. "Those baby clothes were for Rosita."

Colleen grinned. "But isn't it nice that they served your purposes, as well?"

"I am not scheming to plant ideas in Ryan's head," Maggie insisted.

"Oh, really?"

"Really!"

"Well, intended or not, I'm sure it did the trick. I imagine he's thinking of you in a whole new way now."

"Pregnant?" Maggie asked skeptically. "I doubt that. And don't you think it's a giant leap, anyway? He hasn't even so much as asked me out on a date."

"But you want him to," Colleen guessed.

Maggie thought of the way she felt every time Ryan's blue-eyed gaze settled on her. "Yes, I want him to. He's a very mysterious, complicated man, and you know how I enjoy unraveling a puzzle."

"And if he doesn't ask you out?"

Maggie shrugged. "He owns a pub. I can pretty much see him whenever I want to."

Colleen seemed surprised by her response. "You would do that? You'd just hang around the pub until he notices you?"

"I might. It's a great place. You should have come in with me just now. Even at this hour the jukebox was playing and there were groups of people laughing."

"I figured three would be a crowd."

"Well, if you had come in, you'd know what I'm talking about. I felt right at home there the second I walked in the other night. It's not like some sleazy bar. It's just the way Mom and Dad have always described the pubs in Ireland."

"I can't wait to hear what Mom and Dad are going to have to say about this. You know how Dad always warned us to steer clear of bars."

"You'll never meet the man of your dreams in a bar," they both said in a chorus.

Maggie laughed. "How could I forget? But how can they object with Father Francis sitting right there most evenings? Besides, didn't you pay attention to what I said not five seconds ago? This is a pub, not a bar—there's a difference."

"I hope you don't mind if I sit in while you try explaining that to Dad," Colleen said.

"Dad's already well aware of the difference, so I won't even try explaining it to him. Besides, I've always believed in being honest with Mom and Dad about what I'm doing, and expecting them to trust my judgment. They usually do."

"So when are you going back? Tonight?"

Maggie shook her head. "Even *I* know that's too soon. I thought I'd give Ryan a day or two to wonder what's happened to me. I'm thinking I'll go back the first of the week. Want to come along for a girls' night out?"

"Something tells me Daniel would object to baby-sitting so I could go hang out with you while you try to pick up a man. If you need a chaperone, take Katie."

Maggie thought of the way her sister had practically swooned at the sight of Ryan. "Never mind."

Colleen shot a knowing look at her. "She's your sister. She would never try to steal your guy."

"It's not her I'm worried about. Have you taken a good look at our baby sister? She's gorgeous, something she doesn't even realize."

"And you think Ryan might prefer her?" Colleen asked. "Come on, Mags. He never even gave her a second glance yesterday."

Maggie regarded her sister with surprise. "He didn't?"

"Sweetie, he never took his eyes off you. Didn't you know that?"

Maggie shook her head. “I had no idea. I thought maybe I was fighting an uphill battle.”

“You may be,” Colleen warned. “He doesn’t strike me as someone who wants to fall in love. He may not even believe in it.”

“That’s what Father Francis said, as a matter of fact,” Maggie admitted.

“Well then, at least you know what you’re up against. But a powerful attraction has a way of making a man take risks he never intended. It’s all a matter of patience and persistence.”

“I was blessed with one—” she thought of her total lack of patience “—but definitely not the other.”

“Then Ryan promises to be good for you in more ways than one, doesn’t he? Just keep reminding yourself—if he’s the one, then he’s worth waiting for.”

“You might have to do the reminding,” Maggie said.

Her sister chuckled. “Oh, sweetie, that will be my pleasure.”

Throughout what seemed like the longest weekend on record, Ryan’s gaze kept drifting toward the door each time it opened. He kept expecting—hoping—to see Maggie coming in with each blast of icy air. He was so obvious that there was little chance that Father Francis or Rory hadn’t taken note of him doing it, but they’d remained oddly silent.

Monday the pub was closed. That was the day Ryan usually spent running errands and catching up on paperwork, but he couldn't seem to concentrate today. He finally gave up in disgust around four-thirty and headed out to take a brisk walk to clear his head. Maybe that would push images of Maggie out of it.

Instead, when he opened the door, he bumped straight into her. He stood there staring like an awkward teenager. "Maggie, what are you doing here?"

She swallowed hard and backed up a step. "I came by for a cup of coffee or two. I'm freezing."

"The bar's closed today, but I'd be happy to fix you one," Ryan said, stepping aside to let her in.

"Closed?" she asked blankly.

He grinned. "As in not open for business," he explained patiently. He pointed toward the carved wooden sign posted by the door, where it plainly stated that the pub was closed on Mondays.

"Oh," she said, her cheeks flaming. "I never even looked at the sign. I just assumed, I guess, that you were open every day, but of course you'd need time off. I'll come back another time." She whirled around.

"Maggie?"

"Yes."

"I thought you were freezing."

She faced him with a defiant lift of her chin. "It's nothing. I'll just turn up the car heater."

He should let her go. He certainly shouldn't be inviting her in when there was no one around to serve as a buffer, no other customers needing his attention. Still, he found himself saying, "I wouldn't mind having some coffee myself. I was going for a walk to clear the cobwebs out of my head, but coffee will accomplish the same thing." Never mind that he'd already drunk gallons of it and Maggie was the only thought cluttering his brain.

She beamed at him. "Well, if you're sure."

Ryan wasn't sure of anything, not when she looked at him like that. "Come on in," he said, "before it's as cold inside as out."

When she was in, he closed the door and flipped the lock, then retreated behind the bar. He figured it would give him the illusion of safety, maybe keep him from reaching for her and kissing her until her cheeks flamed pink from something other than the chilly air.

When he'd fixed a fresh pot of coffee and poured two cups, he handed one to her, then took a sip of his own.

"Do you need to stay behind the bar?" she asked. "Can't you come out here and sit next to me? Or maybe we could go to one of the booths?"

"I'm fine here," he said. "This is where I'm used to being."

"And we definitely wouldn't want to drag you

out of your comfort zone," she said, her eyes sparkling with undisguised amusement.

He scowled at that. "There are reasons why people have comfort zones," he said. "Why mess with them?"

"It's called living," she pointed out. She patted the bar stool next to her. "Come on, Ryan. Take a risk. We'll save the cozy booth for another day."

He sighed and gave in to the inevitable. He walked around the bar, but when he sat, he carefully left one stool between them. She bit back a grin.

"Oh, well, that's progress anyway," she teased. "No need to rush things."

"Maggie, why are you here? It's not as if this is the only place in town where you can get a coffee."

"But it's the only place where I know the owner," she said. "By the way, since you are the owner and it's your day off, what are you doing here?"

"Catching up on this and that," he said evasively.

"Doesn't sound like much of a day off to me. Have you ever heard of taking a real break?"

"To do what?" he asked, genuinely baffled.

She regarded him with blatant pity. "Whatever you want."

"I want to catch up on all the things I don't get to do when this place is busy," he said defensively. "Paperwork, bookkeeping, checking supplies."

Maggie shook her head. "Don't you have a hobby?"

"No."

"Something you enjoy doing to relax?" she persisted.

Uncomplicated sex relaxed him, but Ryan seriously doubted she wanted to hear about that. And today sex had been the last thing on his mind. Okay, not exactly true, he mentally corrected. Sex with Maggie had been very much on his mind, which he'd concluded was a really, really bad idea.

Even so, he couldn't quite keep himself from giving her a blatant once-over that had her blushing.

"Not that," she said, evidently grasping his meaning with no trouble at all.

"Too bad," he teased. "I do find that relaxes me quite a bit."

Her gaze locked with his. "Perhaps another time," she said in a deliberately prim little voice.

Ryan choked on the sip of coffee he'd just taken. "What did you say?" When she started to reply, he cut her off. "Never mind. Let's not go there."

Now it was her turn to regard him with a knowing look. "Oh? Why is that?"

"Maggie, what do you want from me?" He couldn't seem to prevent the helpless, bewildered note in his voice.

Her expression faltered at the direct question. “Honestly?”

He nodded.

“I’m not entirely sure,” she replied, as if she found the uncertainty as disconcerting as he did.

“Then you’re playing a risky game,” he warned.

“I know,” she agreed, meeting his gaze. “But I can’t seem to stop myself. I keep finding myself drawn here. There’s something about this place, about you . . .” Her voice faltered and she shrugged. “I can’t explain it.”

Gazes locked, they both fell silent. Finally Maggie sighed and looked away.

“Can I ask you something?” she said eventually, still not meeting his gaze.

“Sure.”

“Father Francis told me something. He said that you don’t believe in love.”

“Father Francis has a big mouth, but he’s right. I don’t,” Ryan said grimly.

“Why?”

Rather than answering, he said, “I gather you do believe in it. Why?”

“Because I see it every single day. I see it between my parents. I’ve felt their love since the day I was born. I see it with my brothers and their wives, with Colleen and her husband. There’s nothing they wouldn’t do for each other or for their families.”

Ryan listened, trying to put his skepticism

aside. He tried to imagine being surrounded by such examples. He couldn't. His own experience had been the exact opposite. There'd been a time when he'd thought his parents loved him and his brothers, but then they'd vanished without a trace. He'd been forced to question whether their love had ever been real.

"Have you experienced it yourself?" he asked.

"No, but I know it exists because I can feel it just by walking into a room with my family. It's in their laughter, in the way they look at each other, in the way they touch each other. How can you dismiss that when it's right in front of you?"

"No," he said quietly. "It's in front of *you*. I've never seen it."

Because he didn't want to get into a long, drawn-out argument over the existence of love, he deliberately stood up. "I'd better finish running those errands now."

Maggie looked as if she might argue, but then she put down her cup and picked up her coat. "Thanks for the coffee."

"No problem." He jammed his hands in his pockets as he followed her to the door.

She opened the door, then hesitated. This time her gaze clashed with his in an obvious dare. "I'll keep coming back, you know."

An odd sense of relief stole through Ryan at her words—part warning, part promise.

"Unless you tell me to stay away," she challenged, her gaze steady.

"Whatever," he murmured as if the decision were of no consequence.

Her lips curved up. "I'll take that as an invitation."

Before he realized her intention, she stood on tiptoe and pressed her lips to his cheek.

"See you," she said cheerfully, then disappeared down the block before he could gather his thoughts.

Ryan stared into the shadows of dusk, hoping for one last glimpse, but she was gone.

"That was a touching scene," Rory said, stepping out of the shadows.

"Have you been reduced to spying to get your kicks?" Ryan asked irritably.

"Hardly. I just stopped by to see if you'd like a blind date for tonight. My date has a friend. I've met her. She doesn't hold a candle to your Maggie, but I imagine she could provide a much-needed distraction."

"I don't think so," Ryan said. He doubted if both Julia Roberts and Catherine Zeta-Jones rolled into one could distract him tonight.

Rory grinned at him. "Which says it all, if you ask my opinion."

"Which I did not," Ryan said.

"Well, I'm offering it, anyway. A woman like Maggie comes along once in a man's life, if he's lucky. Don't be an idiot and let her get away."

"I don't even know her," Ryan argued. "Neither do you. So let's not make too much of this."

"Are you saying the woman doesn't tie you in knots?"

Ryan frowned at the question. "Whether she does or she doesn't is no concern of yours."

"In other words, yes," Rory interpreted. "So, get to know her. Find out if there's anything more to these feelings. What's the harm?"

Harm? Ryan thought. He could get what was left of his heart broken, that was the harm. Maggie's words came back to him then.

It's called living.

Ryan tried to balance the promise of those words against the reality of the heartbreak he'd suffered years ago and vowed never to risk again. Bottom line? There was nothing wrong with his life just the way it was. It was safe. Comfortable. There were no significant bumps, no nasty surprises.

"See you," he said to Rory. "I've got things to do."

Rory's expression brightened. "You going after her?"

"Nope."

"Why the hell not?"

"Better things to do."

"What could be better than an evening with a beautiful woman?"

"A couple of games of racquetball and an ice-cold beer," Ryan retorted.

Rory laughed. "That's called sublimation, my friend."

"Call it whatever you want to. It's my idea of a great way to spend a few hours."

"That's only because you haven't been on a real date with a woman who might actually matter to you in all the time I've known you," Rory said.

Ryan couldn't deny the accusation. "You live your life. Let me live mine."

"That's the problem, Ryan, me lad. What you're doing's not living, not by any man's definition."

Nor by Maggie's, Ryan was forced to admit. But neither her opinion nor Rory's mattered. His was the only one that counted, and he was perfectly content with his life.

At least he had been till a few days ago, when Maggie O'Brien had blown into the pub on a gust of wind and made it her mission to shatter his serenity. From what he could tell, she was doing a darn fine job of it, too.

Chapter Five

Maggie was beginning to hate the defiantly silent phone at her parents' house. Ryan was definitely not taking the hint. She'd all but thrown herself at him, and he was still maintaining the same aloof, distant air. Without her fairly secure ego, she might have found it humiliating.

If she'd honestly believed that he wasn't the least bit interested in her, she might have accepted that and moved on, but she didn't believe it. Not only did she know Colleen's impression regarding his interest, but her own instincts on her last visit to the pub had told her he was attracted to her. She'd seen the immediate rise of heat in his eyes when he'd found her outside, the too-brief flicker of desire before he'd forced a neutral expression onto his face.

Maybe if she hadn't quit her job, if she had a million things to do, she could have let it go, rather than obsessing about him. The truth was, though, that she was bored with all this time on her hands, and Ryan was the most fascinating element in her life at the moment. The vacation she'd been looking forward to when she'd left Maine was turning tedious. She was not used to being idle. And though she was supposed to be contemplating a future career path, all she could think about was Ryan Devaney. Maybe her personal life had been neglected for too long and needed to be dealt with before she considered her next job.

"What are you frowning about?" her mother asked as she poured herself a cup of coffee and joined Maggie at the kitchen table. "Or do I need to ask? Is this about Ryan?"

"I know it's ridiculous," Maggie said. "I barely even know the man, but I can't stop thinking about him. He seems so lost and lonely."

Her mother smiled. "Ah, yes, two traits that are guaranteed to fascinate a woman. So, when are you going to do something about it?"

"Such as?"

"Invite him here for dinner."

"Here?" Maggie asked, unable to hide her dismay at the idea of exposing an already jittery Ryan to an inquisition from her parents.

Her mother chuckled at her reaction. "Your father and I are capable of being polite and civilized when necessary," she teased. "Didn't you tell me Ryan had a difficult family background? Maybe being around a normal family would be good for him."

"You think we're normal?" Maggie asked with obvious skepticism.

"Of course I do. A little rambunctious at times, but pretty typical. There are no major dysfunctions I can think of," she added dryly.

"I suppose you're right, but I don't think Ryan

would accept the invitation. Frankly, I think normal makes him uncomfortable. Besides, it's obvious to me that he's happiest on his own turf."

"Meaning the pub," her mother guessed. "Then we'll go to him. I'd like to see this young man of yours again. How about tonight? Your father should be home early, and since it's Friday, neither of us has to work tomorrow. It's been ages since we've had a night out in Boston."

The prospect of descending on Ryan's Place with Nell and Garrett O'Brien in tow made Maggie decidedly uneasy, but her family was a big part of her life. She might as well find out now if Ryan could cope with that.

"Are you sure?" she asked her mother.

"Of course I'm sure. It's a great excuse to spend the evening out with my husband. And didn't you say there's an Irish band at the pub on weekends? That will be lovely," she said, then quickly amended, "as long as we can keep your father away from the microphone."

Maggie grinned. Her father's enthusiasm for singing was a family legend. Sadly, though, he couldn't carry a tune, but that had never kept him silent.

"Keeping Dad away from the stage will be your job," she told her mother. "I can't have Ryan threatening to bar us from the premises."

Her mother chuckled. "Yes, that would pretty much ruin your grand scheme, now wouldn't it?"

• • •

Ryan had been lured over to the homeless shelter by a frantic call from Father Francis. When he arrived, he found the priest trying to console a heavyset African-American woman who was clutching a crying boy about ten years old. As he got closer he could see that the boy had some sort of medical problem that had left his complexion ashen and his eyes listless.

When Father Francis spotted Ryan, he gave the woman's hand a pat, then left her to join Ryan.

"What's the problem?" Ryan asked.

"That poor woman is beside herself, and who could blame her?" the priest said. "A few weeks ago the doctors told her that her son has a congenital heart problem that requires surgery. He also mentioned that it's probably something he inherited from his father. Apparently, the news was so distressful for the father that he quit his job and took off, leaving them with no income and no insurance."

Ryan felt his gut tighten with knee-jerk anger at a man who would do that to his family. He pushed the reaction aside to deal with the real crisis. "I suppose you want money for the surgery," he said. "I'll make the arrangements tomorrow. You could have told me about it tonight at the pub. Why bring me over here?"

"Because that boy needs his father," the priest said. "He can't go into such a risky surgery believing that his own father doesn't care about him. Though you never faced a major illness, I'm sure you can relate to how he must be feeling."

Unfortunately, Ryan could relate to it all too well. "You can't expect me to find his father."

"I do." Father Francis regarded him with a steady look. "I think your own experience will motivate you to help. And if finding his father can't be accomplished in a matter of days, then I want you to step in and be his friend."

Ryan had no difficulty offering financial assistance, even in hiring a private detective to conduct a search, but involving himself emotionally in the boy's situation was out of the question. "What's wrong with *you* being his friend?" he asked testily.

"I'm a priest, and I'm an old man. It wouldn't be the same," Father Francis insisted. "Come. Meet the boy and his mother. You'll need to talk to them to get the information you'll need for the search."

"You're assuming I'll go along with this," Ryan grumbled.

"Well, of course you will," Father Francis said without a trace of doubt. "That's the kind of man you are. You put aside your own feelings to do what's needed for someone else."

Ryan was growing weary of living up to such high expectations, but he dutifully followed the priest. The woman watched their approach with a wary expression.

"Letitia Monroe, this is Ryan Devaney. He's here to help." Father Francis patted the boy's hand. "And this is Lamar."

Ryan nodded at the mother and shook the child's icy hand. "Nice to meet you, Lamar. You, too, Mrs. Monroe."

"You can help us find my husband?" she asked, her cheeks still damp with tears.

"I'll see what I can do," Ryan promised. "I have some friends who are pretty good at finding people who are missing."

She looked alarmed at his words. "Not the police," she said urgently.

"No, not the police," he reassured her. He hunkered down so he could look Lamar in the eyes. "You a Celtics fan?"

The boy's eyes lit up. "They're the greatest," he said, his voice weak.

Ryan had to steel himself not to feel anything, not pity, not anger. "Well, once you've had your surgery, we'll see about getting you tickets to a game. Would you like that?"

"Really?" Lamar whispered.

"That's a promise. Now let me talk to your mom for a minute. Father Francis will keep you company. Just don't play checkers with him," he warned, then confided, "he cheats."

"What a thing to say about your priest," Father

Francis scolded, but there was a twinkle in his eyes.

Ryan spent a few minutes with Mrs. Monroe, trying to garner enough facts to pass along to a private investigator who visited the pub most evenings on his way home.

"Do you really think you can find him?" Mrs. Monroe asked. "It will mean the world to Lamar to have his daddy at his side when he has this surgery."

"And to you, I imagine," Ryan suggested.

"Me?" she scoffed. "I don't care if I ever set eyes on his sorry behind again. What kind of man runs out on his family at the first sign of trouble?"

Ryan couldn't think of any acceptable excuse for it, either, but he tried. "Father Francis said Lamar's condition could be hereditary. Perhaps your husband simply feels guilty."

She seemed startled by the suggestion. "You think that's it?"

"I don't know your husband, Mrs. Monroe. You do. But if it were me, I'd be struggling with a lot of emotions about now. Maybe you should wait till you talk to him before you give up on him."

She nodded slowly. "I'll think about what you said. And I'm grateful for whatever you can do."

"Let's pray I'll be back to you with some news in a day or two. In the meantime, you make the arrangements for Lamar's surgery. You won't have any problem at the hospital."

"But they said—"

He met her gaze. "Trust me. There won't be a problem."

A relieved smile spread across her face. "Mr. Devaney, I don't know how to thank you."

"There's no need," he insisted, casting a look toward the boy who was giggling softly at something Father Francis had said. "Let's just make sure Lamar is back on his feet soon. I'm looking forward to going to that ball game with him."

Before he knew it, he was enveloped in a fierce hug.

"You'll be in my prayers every night of my life," she told him.

"I'd return the favor, but I think you'll have better luck letting Father Francis do the honors," he said wryly. "I've got to get back to work now, but I'll be in touch. You can count on it."

Ryan slipped out of the shelter before Father Francis could waylay him with some other mission of mercy. Outside, he shivered, though it was less a reaction to the temperature than to the sad plight of the Monroe family.

He was still thinking about them when he walked into the pub and headed for the bar, where Maureen had been filling in while he was gone.

"Everything okay?" she asked, regarding him with concern.

"It will be," he said with grim determination. "Has Jack Reilly been in tonight?"

"Haven't seen him," she said. "But there *is* a familiar face in that booth by the stage."

"Oh?" he said, puzzled by the mysterious glint of amusement in her eyes. One glance at the booth was explanation enough. Maggie was seated there with her parents. They each had the night's fish-and-chips special and a pint of ale. He glanced at Maureen. "Cover for me a few more minutes?"

"Of course," she said at once.

He walked across the room, greeting several regulars along the way, then paused beside Maggie. "Good evening. Welcome to Ryan's Place," he said, his gaze directed first at Nell O'Brien, then at her husband. He nodded at Maggie.

"Ryan, I love your pub," Nell said with enthusiasm. "It reminds me of a place in Dublin that Garrett and I visited on our honeymoon."

"The Swan," Garrett said at once. He regarded his wife with a warm expression. "I believe we can credit a night there for our firstborn son."

Nell blushed. "Garrett O'Brien, what a thing to be saying in front of a stranger."

"Ryan's no stranger. He's a friend of our Maggie's. Isn't that right, Maggie, me girl?"

Maggie grinned at her father. "He still might prefer not to know all the intimate details of John's conception."

Ryan chuckled. "Actually I'm fascinated," he

said, just to keep the color high in her cheeks. "And what about Maggie's? Is there a story behind that, as well?"

Maggie shot a warning look at her father. "If you tell it, I will never forgive you."

"Now I really am intrigued," Ryan said. "Make room, Maggie." He settled in the booth beside her, thigh-to-thigh, in a way that had his blood heating. "Come on, Mr. O'Brien. Tell the story."

Garrett O'Brien opened his mouth, then grunted, apparently when Maggie's foot made contact with his shin. "Sorry, lad. I've been persuaded to keep silent. Even in today's tell-all society, I imagine there are some things that are best kept private."

Ryan turned to Maggie. "I suppose I'll just have to pester you until *you* tell all," he said. "Right now, though, I'd better get behind the bar before Maureen rebels." And before he gave in to the urge to spend the entire evening right here with Maggie so close he could feel her breath on his cheek when she spoke.

"Join us again if you can spare the time," Nell invited.

"I'll do that," Ryan promised, casting a last, lingering look at Maggie before striding across the room and trying to block her presence from his thoughts.

He didn't get to keep his promise. Instead, it turned into an impossibly long night. Fridays were always busy because of the popularity of the band, but this was busier than most. It didn't help that his new waiter was struggling a bit to keep up with the unfamiliar orders, but Ryan had to give Juan credit for trying. Still, it meant that Maureen was carrying more than her fair share of the load and that Ryan was spending extra time soothing ruffled feathers and keeping an eye out for Jack Reilly so he could ask for his help in tracking down Lamar's father.

Suddenly Maggie was beside him. "It looks as if you could use an extra pair of hands behind the bar," she said, already donning an apron.

He stopped filling an order for ale from the tap and stared. "What are you doing?"

"Pitching in," she said, moving away to smile at a new arrival. She'd taken the man's order and placed a pint of ale in front of him before Ryan could blink. She came back to him with a satisfied smile on her face. "Any objections?"

Ryan weighed uneasiness against pragmatism. Pragmatism won. "Not a one," he said. "I can use the help."

Just then he spotted her parents heading toward the door. They gave him a cheery wave as they exited. Gaze narrowed, he turned to Maggie. "Wasn't that your ride home that just walked out of here?"

She grinned at him. "Not if I'm lucky," she said, then vanished to take another order.

"Meaning what?" he said when she reappeared.

"I figure you'll owe me," she said. "A drive home's not too much for a volunteer waitress to expect, is it?"

Ryan shook his head, aware that he'd just fallen into a tidy trap. "No, I suppose not, but I ought to make Rory take you."

Her smile faltered at the suggestion, and Ryan grinned despite himself. "Not what you had in mind, hmm?"

She met his gaze evenly. "Definitely not."

"Then I suppose I'll have to be the one, if only to see exactly where this plan of yours is headed."

"You won't be disappointed," she promised.

She said it with a look that had his temperature soaring.

And a lifetime's worth of defense mechanisms slamming into place.

Maggie figured she would owe her mother for a really long time for coming up with the idea of leaving Maggie behind to help out in the pub. Nell had overcome all of Garrett's objections by reminding him that it would give the two of them several hours at home alone. After that, her father couldn't leave the pub quickly enough. Years of having six children underfoot had taught him to snatch any opportunity for privacy.

Sticking around uninvited had been a risky notion. Ryan could very well have found someone else to give her a lift home, just as he'd threatened. The fact that he'd backed down and decided to take her himself was definitely a good sign. Unfortunately, she wasn't at all convinced they were ever going to get out of the place.

It was past midnight, and the last customer had been gone for twenty minutes, but Ryan was still tallying the receipts, dragging out the process, if she wasn't mistaken. Maggie was sitting in a booth, rubbing her aching feet. It had been a long time since she'd spent so many hours as a waitress and bartender. She'd forgotten how exhausting it could be.

Oddly enough, though, a part of her felt exhilarated. She'd made over fifty dollars in tips, which was the only money she intended to take for her efforts. More important, she had thoroughly enjoyed talking to the customers. She'd missed that kind of interaction with people in her old job. Being the senior accountant for a corporation might have carried more prestige than waiting tables, but it hadn't been nearly as much fun.

She glanced across the room and saw that Ryan had disappeared into his office. Maybe she could hurry him along, if she went over there and looked pathetic, which wouldn't be all that difficult given the way she was feeling.

Groaning, she stood up in her stockinged feet and walked over, carrying her shoes, coat and purse. She found Ryan behind his desk, jotting figures in a ledger.

"I'll be with you in a second," he said without looking up. "I like to get these numbers entered at night, so the day's cleared out and I'm ready to start fresh tomorrow."

"You're keeping your records in a ledger?" she asked, staring at the cumbersome book with surprise. She glanced around the office and saw no evidence of a computer.

"Sure."

"Why aren't you computerized? It would take less time, and you'd have everything you need at your fingertips when tax time comes around."

"This works," he said, dismissing the idea.

"But—"

He glanced up with a grin. "You selling computers in your spare time, too?"

"No, but this is something I know a little bit about. I could set up a system for you in no time. And I noticed tonight that if you reorganized the liquor supply, it would be easier to keep track of what's running low."

"Maggie, I don't need a system. I already have one," he explained patiently.

"An outdated one, but I suppose that's to be expected," she said.

He frowned at that. "Meaning?"

"You're pretty much stuck in your ways across the board," she said.

For a minute it seemed he might take offense, but then he grinned. "It must seem that way to you, being the kind of modern woman that you are."

"It *is* that way," she insisted, ignoring the teasing. "But I won't push you to change tonight. I'm too exhausted to waste the energy." She grinned back at him. "But, as they say, tomorrow is another day."

"I'm *not* changing the way I do things around here," he said emphatically.

"We'll see," she said blithely.

"Maggie!"

"Don't worry about it," she soothed. "I'll just sit right over here, quiet as a mouse, while you finish up. You won't even know I'm here."

"I doubt that," he muttered.

She settled into the easy chair in the corner of his office, curling her feet up under her. Two minutes later she was sound asleep.

Ryan compared his figures one last time, then uttered a sigh of satisfaction. The orderliness of numbers pleased him. There was nothing messy or questionable about totals written down in black and white. Emotions, however, were another matter entirely.

And speaking of emotions, what was he to do about Maggie? He glanced across the room and found her sound asleep in his easy chair. At some point during the evening, she'd scooped her hair into some sort of ponytail, but there were curls escaping now to feather against her cheeks. Her dark-green sweater had twisted and ridden up to expose a tantalizing inch-wide strip of pale-as-cream skin. His heart hammered a little harder at the sight. If only he had the right to skim a finger along that delicate band of flesh, to slide his hand beneath the sweater to cup softly rounded breasts. His throat went dry at the thought.

He swallowed hard. He had to get her out of here and safely home before he did something stupid and acted on one of these increasingly frequent impulses of his.

Crossing the room, he hunkered down beside the chair. Despite his best intentions, he couldn't seem to resist reaching out to smooth a wayward curl from her cheek, then lingering to feel the way her skin heated at his touch.

"Maggie?" he whispered, his voice suddenly husky. "Time to wake up."

She moaned softly and stirred, but didn't open her eyes. Ryan bit back a groan as images of her stirring just like that in his bed slammed through him. Visions of tangled sheets falling away from long, bare legs taunted him.

"Maggie," he repeated with more urgency. "Time to go home."

He said the latter to remind himself that home was where she belonged—her home, not his.

Another moan. Another stretch. And then a sigh as her eyes flickered open. A smile curved her lips. "Hi," she said softly.

"Hey, sleepyhead."

"I guess I fell asleep. What time is it?"

"After one. I need to get you home."

She kept her gaze steady on him. "I could stay here. Save you the trip."

Ryan stood up and backed away so fast he nearly tripped over his own feet. "Not a good idea."

She seemed amused by his reaction. "Surely you have a sofa I could sleep on," she said, her expression innocent. "Where do you live, by the way?"

"Upstairs."

"Well then, that's a whole lot handier than driving all the way to my place."

"Maybe so, but something tells me I don't want to tangle with your father and your brothers, who might find the idea of you staying at my place a little premature."

She grinned. "Premature, not out of the question?"

"Maggie." It came out as part protest, part plea.

"I just want things to be absolutely clear between us," she said.

"And I'll be happy to let you know when I have them figured out," Ryan retorted.

"You're assuming you're the only one who gets to have a say," she accused lightly. "Wrong, Devaney. I'm part of this equation."

"Didn't you tell me that your life is in a bit of a muddle right now?" he asked. "You don't need to add to that by getting mixed up with me."

She rose gracefully from the chair and crossed the room until she could reach up and place a hand against his cheek. Ryan felt that touch straight through to his toes.

"What if I want to get mixed up with you?" she asked.

"Why would you want that? I'm not an easy man to be with, Maggie. I don't let people in. I like my privacy. I like the status quo."

She laughed. "If that was supposed to scare me off, it missed the mark.You've just made the game more interesting."

"Is that all it is to you, a game? Because if that's it, maybe we have something to talk about after all. But if it's more you're after—" he captured her gaze and held it "—I'm the wrong man."

Her gaze never faltered. "I suppose time will tell about that, won't it?"

She stood on tiptoe and touched her lips to his, a quick brush of soft heat that invited more. Too much more.

Before Ryan could stop himself, he'd dragged her back for another kiss, this one deeper and more urgent. He was only dimly aware of the soft-as-satin texture of her mouth under his, of the faint taste of coffee and the heady scent of perfume. What truly captured his attention was the jolt to his system, the rush of blood and lick of fire that had him wanting more . . . needing more. Her body—soft and pliant—molded to his, as close as a second skin, as tempting and dangerous as anything he'd ever known.

He was on the brink of dragging her straight upstairs, not to his sofa but to his bed, when reason kicked in. Breathing hard, he backed away and dragged a shaky hand through his hair.

"I'm sorry," he apologized.

"I'm not," she said, sounding more triumphant than shaken. "I've been waiting my whole life for a kiss like that."

Warning bells went off in Ryan's head. "It was just a kiss," he said, regarding her uneasily.

"That's like saying the Revolutionary War was just a little disagreement over tea."

Despite his wariness, the analogy amused him. "There was the Boston Tea Party," he reminded her.

"Tip of the iceberg," she countered. "It's okay, though, if this was just a kiss for you. Maybe then you won't mind doing it again."

He heard the teasing note in her voice and decided to ignore the challenge. "Not tonight. Grab your coat and let's get out of here."

"Chicken," she murmured as she passed him.

"Damn straight," he replied without apology. Anything else and he'd be making the kind of decisions a man would only live to regret.

Chapter Six

When Maggie finally crept into the house, it was nearly three in the morning. No sooner had she crossed the threshold into the kitchen, though, than the light was switched on. Maggie nearly jumped out of her skin.

"A little late, aren't you?" Katie inquired, looking thoroughly pleased at having scared the daylights out of her big sister.

"What are you doing up?" Maggie asked irritably. "Come to think of it, what are you doing *here?* I thought you'd gone back to your own place."

"Since my big sister's visiting, I thought I'd spend some time at home," Katie said. "Imagine my surprise when I arrived and found that no one was home. I waited for hours before Mom and Dad got here."

Maggie thought of her parents' delight at the prospect of going home to be alone. "I'm sure they were thrilled to find you here," she said dryly.

Katie frowned. "Actually, they did seem a bit taken aback. What was that about?"

Maggie smothered a grin. "Just think about it, okay?" She glanced at Katie's mug of hot chocolate. "Is there more of that?"

"There are packages in the cabinet. I zapped it

in the microwave." When Maggie shuddered, she added, "Dump enough marshmallows on the top and you can't tell the difference." She stood up. "Here, I'll do it. You sit down and put your feet up. You look beat. What did you do tonight?"

"Mom and Dad didn't tell you?"

"They made some cryptic remark about you being with Ryan."

"That's right. Actually, I helped out at the pub."

Katie paused with the cup halfway into the microwave and stared. "I thought you swore you would never wait tables again after you worked out at the Cape that summer during college."

"This was different."

Katie grinned. "Because Ryan was there," she guessed. "Ah, the things we do for love."

"I'm not in love with him," Maggie protested. She was fascinated, curious, in lust . . . but love? No way. She might believe in it, but she wanted to get the rest of her life in order first.

"Just halfway there?"

"Not even halfway," Maggie insisted, though the memory of that bone-melting kiss they'd shared sent heat shimmering through her all over again. "He's an attractive man and a decent, complicated guy. I want to get to know him."

"In the carnal sense, I imagine," Katie said slyly.

"Katie O'Brien, you shouldn't say such things," Maggie protested indignantly.

“Well, if you don’t, you’re crazy.” She handed Maggie the mug of nuked chocolate with four marshmallows jammed on top.

“Let’s drop the topic of Ryan Devaney for the moment,” Maggie said. “What about you? With everyone around, we hardly had a chance to talk over Thanksgiving. Any man in your life?”

“Not even one on the horizon,” Katie said. “It makes Dad very happy.”

“But you like your job, right? You’re happy teaching?”

Katie grinned. “I love the kids, even if Dad does think that teaching kindergarten is little more than glorified baby-sitting. They’re so eager to learn at that age. And the school is small enough that I can really get to know each child and figure out the best way to get through to him.”

“You’re more like Mom than any of the rest of us. You have endless patience and a real knack for making learning fun.”

“Thanks,” her sister said, clearly pleased by the praise. “But it’s going to be way too easy to wind up in a rut. Next thing I know, I’ll be forty and single and wondering what happened. It doesn’t help that most of the people I know these days are female teachers and moms.”

“Oh, please,” Maggie scoffed. “I don’t think you need to worry about that yet.”

Katie regarded her with a knowing expression. “Isn’t that what brought you home? Didn’t you wake up one day and realize that you were dissatisfied with your life?"

Maggie thought about it. "In a way, I suppose. I wasn't meeting interesting people, and the work was boring. I wasn't making use of half the skills I learned when I got my MBA. I needed a new challenge."

"Like I said, you were dissatisfied. Any idea what you'll do next? Will you go back to Maine?"

"I've kept the house for the time being, but I don't know. It's going to be hard to find the kind of work I really want."

"Which is?"

"Something where I can make better use of my degree and my people skills."

"Like running a pub?" Katie inquired slyly.

Maggie laughed, thinking of her earlier attempt to convince Ryan to update his accounting methods or even to reorganize his inventory. "If I decide on that, I suspect I'll have to find someplace other than Ryan's," she said wryly. "He balks at the prospect of changing the least little thing."

Katie laughed. "You've already tried, haven't you? What did you do, start messing with his accounting procedures?"

"I just recommended that he consider computerizing his bookkeeping."

"And he told you to buzz off?"

"More or less."

"So, of course, the next time you go, you'll take along a few sample spreadsheets and show him how simple it would be," Katie guessed.

Maggie took the joking suggestion seriously. "Actually, not a bad idea."

"Oh, Mags," Katie said with a shake of her head. "Telling a man he's doing something all wrong is not the way to win his heart. Of course, maybe you'd rather have a job than his heart."

"Why does it have to be an either-or situation?"

"Because he's a man," Katie said wisely.

Maggie sighed. "He is definitely that."

Katie regarded her speculatively. "Have you kissed him?"

At Maggie's blush, she hooted. "You have, haven't you? Was it great?"

"Oh, yes," Maggie murmured. "Better than great."

"Then forget about the man's financial system. Concentrate on what's important."

"And that would be?"

"If you don't know," Katie said with a pitying expression, "then nothing I can say will help."

She stood up, gave Maggie a peck on the cheek and announced, "I'm going to bed. You coming?"

Maggie shook her head. "Not just yet."

A worried frown creased Katie's brow. "Mags, don't analyze this to death."

"More advice from the woman who doesn't have a man in her life?"

“Yes,” Katie said, her expression serious. “Take it from someone who analyzed the love of her life right out the door.”

She swept out of the room before an open-mouthed Maggie could comment. This was the first Maggie had heard about her baby sister losing the man of her dreams. Had anyone in the family known? As far as Maggie knew, everyone had assumed Katie was happily playing the field, years away from wanting to settle down, just as their father preferred. Apparently, they were all wrong. None of them had even suspected that she’d met the man of her dreams, much less lost him.

Adding worry about Katie’s unexpected revelation to her already churning thoughts about Ryan’s kiss, Maggie concluded it was going to be a very long night.

Since Jack Reilly hadn’t stopped by the pub on Friday night, Ryan set out to track him down first thing Saturday morning. He was actually relieved to have something to do that might keep his mind off of Maggie, at least for a couple of hours. He doubted there was anything that could banish her from his thoughts permanently, not after that kiss they’d shared.

He found the private investigator on a basketball court a few blocks away, shooting hoops with a bunch of neighborhood kids. When he spotted

Ryan, he passed the ball to one of the boys and loped over to meet him.

"Thank heavens you came along. They were wearing me out," he said, bending down to catch his breath. "Don't know when I got to be so out of shape."

"Too many nights on a barstool?" Ryan asked.

"I don't think a couple of ales account for it. Probably the cigarettes." He grabbed a towel from a bench and wiped his face. "What brings you over here? Were you looking for me?"

Ryan nodded. "I need your expertise." He explained about Letitia Monroe and her son. "Think you can track down the father?"

"If he's using credit cards or gotten a new job, I can probably locate him by the end of the day," Jack said, then held up his hand when Ryan started to say something. "But if somebody really wants to get lost, there won't be much I can do to find them."

"I doubt he gave this enough thought to hide out for long," Ryan said. "I think it was an impulsive decision. He probably just got scared and ran. Sooner or later he'll have to do something for money. They didn't have much. Now Mrs. Monroe and the kid are at the St. Mary's shelter."

One of the boys, taking a break to drink some water, overheard. "You talking about Lamar's dad?"

Ryan nodded. "You know him?"

"Yeah. He used to work with my old man till he quit his job and took off."

"Has your dad mentioned anything about where he might have gone?" Jack asked him.

The boy regarded him warily. "He ain't in no trouble, is he?"

"Not the way you mean," Ryan assured him.

"Then you might try checking around down by the docks. Sometimes you can pick up day work there. My dad said that's what he told him. He said old man Monroe just needed some time to think."

Jack gave the boy a high-five. "Thanks, Rick. I owe you."

"Does that mean you'll give me another lesson on that fancy computer of yours?" the boy asked hopefully.

"Meet me at my place at five. I can spend an hour or so with you then," Jack promised.

A grin split the boy's face. "All right!"

Jack shook his head as the gawky kid, who kept tripping over his own feet, moved back onto the basketball court. "Never seen a kid so eager to learn. I find him on my doorstep half a dozen times a week, hoping I'll show him how to do things on the computer. He's getting so he can do a search and turn up things I never even thought to look for. Pretty soon, *he'll* be giving *me* lessons."

"You think there's anything to his suggestion

about looking for Lamar's dad down by the docks?"

"No way of telling till I go down there. I'll go now, then stop by the pub and let you know what I find out. When's the kid's surgery?"

"It's not scheduled yet, but I imagine it'll be in the next week or two. It's a risky procedure. The boy needs to know his father's there for him."

"Then we'll find a way to make that happen," Jack said confidently.

"You need a retainer?" Ryan asked.

"No way. This one's on me. Just make sure there's a cold ale waiting for me when I get there later."

"Thanks, Jack."

"Hey, not a problem. I can't have the neighborhood thinking you're the only good guy around. I need my share of those babes who are always circling around you. Hell, I'd even take one of Rory's rejects."

Ryan laughed. "You pick out any woman in the pub and I'll introduce you."

"I saw a redhead in there the night before Thanksgiving . . ." Jack began.

Ryan stiffened. "Except her," he said.

Jack's gaze narrowed. "What's up with that? Is she married?"

"No."

"Engaged?"

"No."

A grin spread across Jack's face. "Yours?"

Ryan hesitated, then sighed. "Could be." Whether he wanted it that way or not.

Maggie walked into the pub shortly after three in the afternoon lugging a laptop, a portable printer and a package of paper. Rory came out of the kitchen, took one look at her and rushed over to take some of the load.

"You trying to get a hernia?" he demanded. "What is all this stuff?"

"I wanted to make a point with Ryan. Is he around?"

"He went by the shelter. He should be back soon." He paused in the middle of the room. "Where do you want this?"

"In his office," she said at once.

Rory shook his head. "I don't think that's such a good idea."

"Why not?"

"Nobody goes in Ryan's office without an invitation."

"Why is that?"

"Because he says so," Rory said simply. "And since something tells me he's not going to be real happy to see all this fancy technological stuff, anyway, maybe you better not start off on the wrong foot by busting in there when he's not around."

Maggie considered the advice. "You could

have a point. Set it on the end of the bar. There's bound to be a plug nearby."

Rory shook his head again. "If I were you, I'd pick a real dark corner."

Maggie laughed. "The bar will do."

He shrugged. "Suit yourself. Hope you don't mind if I go back in the kitchen. I want to be out of the line of fire when he gets back. Can I get you a drink or something before I go?"

"No, thanks. Besides, I worked the bar last night. If I get thirsty, I can fix something."

A look of delight split his round face. "Taking over here, are you? That's the girl. Poor Ryan's head must be spinning."

She grinned at that. "I certainly hope so."

"Well, I'll leave you to it, then. You need any advice from a man who knows him well, you come to me. There's little about Ryan Devaney that I don't know. He's the best friend a man could have. And something tells me if a woman can win his heart, he'll be the best husband, as well. The trick lies in the winning. You won't do it overnight."

"I'll keep that in mind," Maggie said, finding it interesting that Rory's impression so closely mirrored Father Francis's.

While she waited for Ryan to arrive, she set up the computer and printer, then opened her business finance program. She began filling in all the inventory categories she could think of for a pub. Satisfied that she'd hit on most of them, she looked up to find Ryan standing over her, a scowl on his face.

"What's this?" he inquired, as if she'd brought a dangerous foreign object into his pub.

"A free demonstration," she said cheerfully. "Come see."

"I don't have the time. I've a business to run. And I'm getting a late start as it is."

"What I'm suggesting would make it easier," she said.

"Can it serve drinks?"

She frowned at the mocking question. "No, but—"

"Then I'm not interested," he said flatly. He reached for an apron and tied it around his waist, then vanished to the far end of the bar, leaving her to stare after him.

"Don't mind Ryan," Father Francis advised, appearing out of nowhere and sliding onto the stool next to her. "He'll come around. After a childhood that was filled with the unexpected, he works hard to keep things steady and familiar, now that he's grown. It takes him a while to warm up to new people and even longer to listen to new ideas."

"And I'm pushing at the boundaries of his comfort zone," Maggie assessed thoughtfully, considering his reaction from a fresh perspective. "Maybe I should back off."

"Now, why would you be wanting to do such a thing?" Father Francis demanded. "Change is what keeps us all alive. Ryan does too little of it."

"If you're so fond of change, why don't you invite her over to the church to meddle in your business?" Ryan inquired sourly as he plunked an Irish coffee down in front of the priest. "I imagine you have ancient systems there that could use an overhaul."

"Perhaps I will," Father Francis said readily. "In fact, I think I'll see if we have the budget for it. Would you be interested, Maggie?"

Maggie was more interested in the fact that Ryan's expression turned even darker at the priest's acceptance of his challenge. Still, she turned to Father Francis. "I'd be happy to take a look and see if I have any suggestions," she told him. "The consultation's on the house. After that, we'll see if there's anything I can contribute, and discuss terms."

"Well, isn't that just perfect?" Ryan snapped, retreating to the opposite end of the bar, where he slammed a few mugs around so hard, it was amazing that they didn't shatter.

Maggie sighed. "I'd better talk to him. I owe him an apology for pushing so hard."

"No, child," Father Francis said at once. "He's the one who needs to apologize. Give him a minute. He'll come around on his own. He knows when he's being unreasonable, and he's generally honest enough to admit it."

Maggie sat back down, but the wait seemed interminable. Finally, though, Ryan approached the two of them with a look of remorse on his face. "Okay, I was out of line." He frowned at the priest. "But you were deliberately pushing my buttons, and you know it."

"Do I now?" Father Francis said, his expression innocent.

"Of course you do. You take great pleasure in it, which makes me wonder why I put up with you." He turned to Maggie. "As for you, I truly am sorry. I know you were trying to be helpful. It's just that I don't need that kind of help. I've been running this place for a while now. I know how to do it. It might not be the most efficient operation, but it works for me."

"And there couldn't possibly be a better way?" she challenged.

He grinned. "There could be, but I'm satisfied with things as they are. When I'm not, I'll let you know."

Maggie knew a brick wall when she slammed into one. "I'll be waiting to hear from you."

"When it comes to this particular topic, you could be in for a long wait," he warned.

"I have the time," she told him.

"And why is that? Shouldn't you be starting that search for a new job?"

"Not just yet. I'm taking the next few weeks to think things through and decide what I want to do. I have an MBA that's going to waste."

He frowned. "Just so you don't get it into your head that this is the place to put it to use," he said. "You're overqualified."

"Okay, okay, I get it. I'll back off," she said, then murmured under her breath, "for now."

He scowled. "I heard that."

Maggie beamed at him. "Just a fair warning," she said cheerfully as she slid off her bar stool.

"You leaving?" he asked.

She grinned at the faint disappointment in his tone. "You should be so lucky. Actually, I'm getting an apron. In case you haven't noticed, the place is packed, and Maureen and Juan have their hands full again."

Ryan shook his head. "A lot of people think a vacation is best spent on a beach in the Caribbean this time of year, not waiting tables in a pub."

"I'm not one of them," she said, grabbing an order pad and heading for a table of couples across the room.

"Bless you," Maureen said as she passed Maggie. "I don't know where everyone came from tonight, but they're all tired and cranky and starving."

"More holiday shopping," Maggie suggested. "And it's only going to get worse when desperation sets in."

"Now there's a cheerful prospect," Maureen said, lifting her gaze heavenward. "Saints protect us from the truly desperate."

Maggie took orders from the three couples, along with a request for the band that was just setting up. She left that and a tip with the lead guitarist, then took the dinner order in to Rory.

The cook beamed when he saw her. "You're still in one piece, I see. Tell me, did you win Ryan over to your way of thinking?"

"Hardly. The man's head is like a rock."

"Aye, that it is. I've been wanting to experiment a bit with the menu, but all of my pleas have fallen on deaf ears," he said, sounding resigned.

"Speaking of changes to the menu, where's Rosita and her recipe for enchiladas?" Maggie asked.

"I sent her home," Rory said.

Maggie regarded him indignantly. "Just like that? She needs the job."

He frowned at her. "Did I say anything about firing her? Her ankles were swelling. And don't you be telling Ryan, either. There's no need for him to dock her pay. As you said yourself, she needs every bit of it to prepare for the baby."

Relieved, Maggie grinned at him. "Why, Rory, I believe the reports of your temper have been greatly exaggerated. You're a softie."

"Only when it comes to mothers-to-be, so don't be getting any ideas about testing my patience," he said. "I expect the wait staff around here to deliver my meals to the tables while they're still hot. Maureen's order's ready. You can take it."

"Yes, sir," she said, loading her tray with the steaming plates and heading for the door.

For the rest of the evening, there was little time for idle chitchat with anyone. As she rushed from table to table, Maggie felt Ryan's steady gaze following her. Just before midnight he nabbed her arm and dragged her to a stool at the end of the bar.

"Sit. Maureen and Juan can handle things from here on out. Have you eaten a bite all evening?" he asked.

"No time," she said, sighing as she kicked off her shoes.

He uttered a sound of disgust and headed for the kitchen. He came back with a plump ham and cheese sandwich and a bowl of Rory's thick potato soup.

"I can't eat at this hour," she protested.

"You can and you will," he said. "I will not be responsible for sending you home half-starved. I won't risk Nell and Garrett's wrath coming down on my head."

Maggie grinned at him. "I'm a grown woman. I take responsibility for my own actions."

"Do they know that? Aren't these the very same parents who worry frantically if you're so much as a few minutes late? Didn't you tell me that yourself on the first night you came through my doors?"

"At least there's one thing I've said that you listened to," Maggie retorted.

"I hear every word out of your mouth," Ryan countered. "I just pick and choose what to ignore." He gestured toward the untouched sandwich. "Now when you've eaten that, I'll drive you home."

"I have my car."

"Then I'll follow you home. It's too late for you to be driving around the streets of Boston all alone. And yes, I know you're a grown woman, but you're not a foolish one. You'll accept my offer and be gracious about it. Otherwise, I'll be the one worrying through the night."

She met his gaze. "Really? You would worry if I drove home alone?"

He sighed heavily. "Yes, really."

Pleased, she relented. "Then you may follow me home, if you agree to come in for coffee when we get there. Deal?" She held out her hand.

Ryan regarded her steadily, reluctance written all over his face. Eventually, though, he clasped her hand in his. "Deal."

It was such a silly, simple agreement, but Maggie felt as if they'd taken a giant leap forward. Now all that remained was to see how many steps backward would follow.

Chapter Seven

Ryan approached the O'Brien house filled with trepidation. He'd expected to find most of the lights off and the family in bed, but instead it looked as if there were a party going on. He said as much when he joined Maggie in the driveway.

"I probably shouldn't intrude," he told her. "It looks as if your parents are entertaining."

"Nonsense," she said, slipping her arm through his. "I imagine some of the family dropped by and they got to playing cards or something. You'll be welcome. Besides, we had a deal. You can't back out now."

It had been a stupid deal. He'd known that when he made it. He should never have agreed to come inside this house where there was so much warmth. It made him yearn for things he'd never had.

He dreaded the prospect of going inside and getting caught up in the kind of teasing camaraderie he'd witnessed when the family had helped out at the homeless shelter. That kind of situation always made him uncomfortable. It caused him to feel more alone, more like an outsider than ever.

He sighed and looked down to find Maggie regarding him with sympathy.

"It will be okay," she reassured him.

"I'll stay long enough for a cup of coffee. That's it," he said. "That was the deal."

"That was the deal," she agreed, leading the way to the kitchen door.

Inside—to his surprise, given the late hour—they found bedlam. Six people were sitting around the kitchen table, poker chips piled in front of them, making enough noise for twenty.

"You cheated," Katie accused her father, barely sparing a glance for Maggie and Ryan as they walked in.

"He most certainly did," one of Maggie's brothers agreed.

Garrett O'Brien rose to his feet, practically quivering with indignation. "The day my own children accuse me of cheating is a sad day, indeed."

"Oh, sit down," Nell ordered. "You did cheat. I saw you myself."

Garrett—most of the fight drained out of him—turned to Ryan for support. "Can you imagine a man's own wife saying such a thing?"

Ryan grinned, his nervousness dissipating. He could imagine Nell O'Brien saying whatever she wanted to whomever she wanted and expecting to be taken seriously. "Well now, I imagine she's a woman who always speaks her mind," he said cautiously, not sure exactly how welcome his opinion might be.

"And always truthfully," Katie added. "Pull up

a chair, Ryan. These guys are just about tapped out. We need deep pockets to join the game."

Ryan felt Maggie's gaze on him.

"Are you willing?" she asked. "Can you stay for a bit?"

Ryan weighed his reluctance against the prospect of a few good poker hands. "I can stay."

"Bring the chairs from the dining room, then," Garrett said. "We'll push over to make room. Maggie, get the man a beer."

"Coffee would be better," Ryan said. "I have to drive back into Boston after this."

"Nonsense," Nell said. "Not when there's a perfectly good guest room that's unoccupied tonight."

"We'll debate that when the time comes," Ryan said, refusing to commit to staying under this roof, especially with the tempting Maggie just down the hall.

Maggie set his coffee in front of him, then slipped onto her own chair right next to him and leaned closer to whisper, "That's the last act of kindness you can expect from me. When it comes to poker, I play a take-no-prisoners game."

"Listen to her," her brother Matt said. "Our Maggie liked to stay up and play with Dad's cronies as she was growing up. Dad allowed it because she split her winnings with him."

Ryan laughed, regarding Maggie with new

respect. "Well, we'll just have to wait and see if you've lost your edge, now won't we?"

"Trust me, there are some things a woman never forgets," she retorted, dealing the cards with quick, professional efficiency.

Ryan drew a scowl from Maggie and hoots from her family when he won the first hand. When it was his turn to deal, he made an elaborate show of allowing her to cut the cards. "For luck," he declared.

"Thank you," she replied, though there was an edge to her polite tone.

"I believe you misunderstood," he said as he dealt. "The lucky cut was for my benefit."

"Oh, my, he's a smug one," Garrett remarked happily.

"With good cause, I'd say," Katie said when she threw in her hand.

Nell, John and Matt followed suit, as did John's wife. Garrett added his cards to the pile with a muffled curse.

Ryan leveled a look into Maggie's eyes. "It looks as if it's just you and me."

Her gaze never wavered. "I'll see your bet and raise you a dollar."

"Uh-oh, our Maggie has that glint in her eyes," Matt said. "Watch yourself, Ryan."

Ryan was already all too aware of the dangers he faced anytime he was around Maggie. This card game was just the tip of the iceberg. "I'll see your raise and call you," he said, watching her expectantly.

"You're absolutely sure you want to do that?" she asked. "There's still time to take it back."

He nodded. "My bet's on the table."

"Okay, then." She fanned her cards out on the table. She had a full house, jacks high.

"Very nice," Ryan complimented her.

She smiled and reached for the pot. "I thought so."

He placed his hand on top of hers. "Just not nice enough." His own full house had kings high.

Maggie frowned as he scooped up the money.

Ryan leaned in close and whispered in her ear, "Don't pout. I told you luck was going to be with me."

Matt winced. "Oh, brother. You've really done it now, Ryan. You've won and, worse, you've gloated about it. She's going to be out for blood."

Maggie gave them all a serene smile. "I am, indeed."

Ryan thought they were joking, but to his amazement Maggie took the next four hands in a row. He regarded her with amusement. "Feeling better now?"

"Much," she said, a satisfied gleam in her eyes.

"Why do I have the feeling this game has gotten personal?" Katie inquired. "I think I'll just slip off to bed while I still have two cents to my name."

"And I have to be getting home before my wife disowns me," Matt chimed in.

John exchanged a look with his wife. "I guess we're out of here, too."

Within ten minutes, the entire room had been cleared. In the silence that followed, Ryan stared at Maggie.

"That was fun," he said.

She seemed surprised. "Even though you lost?"

"Only because I lost to you. You take the game so seriously. Next time, though, I'll know what to watch for. You won't be so lucky."

"What does that mean?"

"It means when you're bluffing, you get this little nervous tic by the corner of your eye. Right about here," he said, touching a finger lightly to her cheek. "And this corner of your mouth starts to tilt up into a smile, but you fight it." He skimmed a caress along her bottom lip to emphasize the point.

Maggie swallowed hard. "Ryan, what are you doing?"

"Just explaining how you give yourself away. I'm surprised the others haven't noticed. Then again, I doubt any of them are as fascinated with your face as I am."

The pulse at the base of her neck jumped. "Ryan . . ." Her voice trailed off.

He leaned forward and covered her mouth with his. He'd been wanting to do that from the moment they'd started to play, had been so obsessed with the idea, in fact, that he'd lost his concentration in the third hand. That was why she'd won so many rounds. His mind hadn't been on the cards at all.

"You taste so good," he whispered against her lips. "And you smell like flowers."

"Roses," she said, sounding breathless. "My favorite perfume."

Shaken by the emotions racing through him, he sat back, sucked in a ragged breath and raked his hand through his hair. "I need to get out of here."

"Mom invited you to stay."

"She wouldn't have, if she'd known what was on my mind," he said.

Maggie's eyes sparkled with curiosity. "Exactly what *is* on your mind?"

"You," he said, opting for total honesty. Maybe that would scare her into being wary around him. "Getting you out of those clothes so I can touch you. Making love to you for the rest of the night."

"Oh, my," she whispered.

He stood up. "Which is why I need to get out of here now."

"No, don't. Stay," she pleaded.

"That's a really bad idea," he said, reaching for his coat.

He leaned down and kissed her one last time. "Good night, Maggie."

"Good night," she said with obvious reluctance.

She stood up and walked with him to the door. "Will you call me when you get home?"

"And wake the household? I don't think so."

"I'll worry if you don't."

He stopped and stared. She'd sounded totally sincere. "You can't be serious," he said, struggling with the unfamiliar sensation her words stirred in him.

"Well, of course I will. It's late. Who knows what could happen on the road at this hour? I'll keep the phone right beside me in the bed. I'll pick up on the first ring. No one else will be disturbed."

It was the first time in decades that anyone had expressed the slightest concern over his whereabouts or his safety. Ryan expected to rebel against it, but instead her plea made him feel warm deep inside. "Okay then, I'll call," he said eventually.

She reached up and touched his cheek. "You're not used to anyone worrying about you, are you?"

"No."

"Well, that's about to change. I'm an O'Brien and we worry about everything," she said lightly.

"Then it's nothing personal?" he said, hiding his disappointment.

"Oh, in your case, it's very personal. I just don't want you freaking out about it."

"I don't freak out."

"Of course you do," she teased. "But that's okay. I understand. You'll get used to me and the others in time."

In time? Ryan wondered about that on the drive back into Boston. Would he ever get used to having someone care what happened to him? Or had his past destroyed any chance of that?

"Who called in the wee hours of the night, or was it morning?" Katie inquired sleepily as the family sat around the breakfast table before church.

"My money's on Ryan," Nell said. Her gaze came to rest on Maggie. "Am I right?"

"I asked him to let me know he made it home safely," she said.

"You couldn't persuade him to stay here?" her mother asked.

"He didn't think it was a good idea," Maggie said.

"Probably afraid we'd catch him sneaking into Maggie's room," Katie said.

"Mary Kathryn O'Brien, watch your tongue," their father scolded. "I don't like to hear such talk from my very own daughter."

Katie refused to be daunted. "Only because you're terrified it could be true and it would ruin forever your image of us as your darling girls, rather than grown-up women."

"That's true enough," he said easily. "And what

is wrong with a man thinking his girls behave as angels, at least until the very day they say their wedding vows?"

"Nothing," Nell soothed. "As long as he's prepared to admit he's been wrong. Now let's drop this before we end up in an argument before mass. Maggie, are you coming with us this morning?"

"I was thinking of going to a mass at St. Mary's," she admitted.

"You think you'll be bumping into Ryan there?" her mother asked.

"I can always hope," Maggie admitted candidly.

"Well, if you do, bring him back with you for Sunday dinner."

"It takes a brave man to face this crowd two days running. I doubt I'll have much luck convincing him, but assuming I see him, I'll try."

Unfortunately, she didn't get the chance. There was no sign of him at the church, but when she ran into Father Francis after mass, he was happy to tell her that Ryan could be found at the shelter. "He likes to spend some time with the children on Sunday morning. I imagine you'll find him with Lamar Monroe this morning."

"Lamar? He hasn't mentioned that name," Maggie said.

"He's a lad Ryan's taken an interest in. He's having surgery later this week."

"I see," Maggie said, sensing there was far

more to the story than Father Francis was sharing. Whatever it was, though, it was also clear she'd have to pry it out of Ryan himself.

She found him, as predicted, sitting on the edge of a cot with a young boy crowded next to him, the boy's fascinated gaze locked on the book Ryan held. Maggie remained in the shadows watching the two of them as Ryan read the story in a voice filled with so much animation that he had the child laughing.

"He's a wonder with my boy," a woman said quietly as she joined Maggie. "I'm Letitia Monroe."

"Maggie O'Brien."

"You're a friend of Ryan's?"

Maggie wondered if she could legitimately make that claim. She asked herself if a few kisses added up to friendship, when it was evident that there was so much about Ryan Devaney that she didn't know.

"I'm hoping to be," she said finally.

Letitia Monroe grinned. "So, that's the way of it, is it? The man is playing hard to get?"

"Try impossible," Maggie said fervently.

"You know what they say about anything worth having," Mrs. Monroe reminded her.

"That it's worth waiting for."

"That's right."

Watching as Ryan coaxed yet another chuckle from the obviously ill boy, Maggie realized with a sudden burst of insight that she would willingly wait for as long as it took.

He looked up then and spotted her. "Hey, Maggie," he said, then turned and said something in an undertone to Lamar that had the boy grinning. Ryan patted a spot next to him. "Come join us. I have to finish reading this story. I can't leave Lamar in suspense."

"Maybe she should do the girl's part," Lamar said. "You sound kind of funny doing it."

"Hey," Ryan protested, "is that any way to treat a man who has humiliated himself to keep you entertained?"

Maggie sat down and reached for the book. "Allow me," she said with a wink at Lamar. She finished reading the last few pages, then sighed as she read, "The end."

"You were real good," Lamar said, approval shining in his eyes.

"Better than me?" Ryan demanded.

Maggie rolled her eyes at the question, causing Lamar to giggle. "Tell him he was better or he'll be grumbling all day," Maggie advised him.

"Mr. Devaney, you were the best," Lamar said dutifully. "Thanks again."

"Anytime, kid. I'll see you before you go to the hospital, okay?"

"Okay," Lamar said, his smile fading. He regarded Ryan fearfully. "You think you're gonna be able to find my dad by then?"

"I'm working on it," Ryan assured him. "I'm going to do everything in my power to make sure he's here with you and your mom before then."

"Thanks. It'll be okay if you don't find him, though. I'm not too scared. And my mom and me will be okay, long as we have each other."

Maggie had to bite her lip to keep from crying at the boy's obvious attempt to appear brave.

"I know that," Ryan told him. "But I'll try hard, just the same." He looked at Maggie. "You ready?"

"Sure." Impulsively, she bent down and gave Lamar a kiss. "You take care of yourself."

"I will. Come back sometime, okay? I wouldn't mind hearing you read another story. My mom doesn't always have the time, and listening is even better than reading to myself."

"I will. I promise."

Outside, Maggie drew in a deep breath. "How risky is this surgery of his?"

"It's heart surgery, so there's bound to be some risk," Ryan said, his expression grim. "It'll go a lot better, though, if he's feeling optimistic."

"Which is why you're trying to track down his dad," she guessed.

Ryan nodded. "He took off when he found out about the surgery. Since he quit his job, that cut off their insurance and their income. That's how they ended up at the shelter."

"Father Francis turns to you a lot in cases like this, doesn't he?"

"He knows I'll do what I can."

"Does it make up for what happened to you?" she asked.

He frowned at the question. "What are you really asking?"

"I notice you're eager to help Lamar find his dad. Have you ever looked for your own?"

She could see the tension in his face as his jaw tightened. "Why the hell would I want to?" he asked heatedly.

"For the same reason you're trying to find Lamar's father for him—because your dad broke your heart when he abandoned you."

Ryan shrugged, clearly refusing to concede the obvious. "I got over it."

"Did you?"

"Yes," he said emphatically, his scowl deepening. "And I don't talk about that time in my life. Not ever."

"Maybe you should."

"And maybe you should mind your own damned business!"

He left her on the sidewalk staring after him, stunned by the force of his anger.

"Well, hell," she muttered, swiping at the tears spilling down her cheeks.

She was still standing in the exact same spot, debating whether to go after him, when Ryan reappeared at the corner. She watched as he sucked in his breath, squared his shoulders and walked toward her.

"I'm sorry," he said. "I shouldn't have bitten your head off like that."

"No," she agreed, "you shouldn't have, even though I understand why you did."

"My family's a sore subject."

"I gathered that."

"Then you won't bring them up again, right?"

She met his gaze evenly and shook her head. "I can't promise that, not when it's so apparent that what happened with them shaped your whole life."

He regarded her with obvious exasperation. "Dammit, Maggie, what do you want from me? You come busting into my life and act as if I'm suddenly your personal mission."

"Maybe that's exactly what you are," she said. "There has to be some reason why I keep coming back to see a man as cranky and ill-tempered as you are."

His lips twitched slightly. "You have a thing for cranky, ill-tempered men?"

"Apparently so," she said with a deliberate air of resignation.

His lips curved into a full-fledged grin then. "Lucky me."

She grinned back at him. "Try to remember that."

"Oh, I imagine you're going to give me plenty of occasions to question it," he said.

She nodded. "It is my mission, remember?"

"Maggie—"

She touched a finger to his lips to silence him. "Just accept it. I'm here to stay."

"But why?" he asked, obviously bewildered.

"It's that cranky, ill-tempered-man thing," she reminded him. "I'm a sucker for a challenge." She hooked her hand around his neck and drew his head down till she could kiss him. "It doesn't hurt that you're a great kisser." She winked at him. "Gotta get home. You're invited for Sunday dinner, by the way. Mom insisted."

He shook his head. "Not today."

"Better things to do?" she asked, not surprised by the refusal and determined not to push for once.

"Nope. Safer things to do," he told her.

Maggie laughed. "See you, then."

She was halfway to her car, rather pleased with herself despite his refusal to come to dinner, when he called after her.

"Hey, Maggie!"

She turned back, regarding him with a questioning look.

"Drive carefully."

"Always do."

"And call me when you get home, okay?"

Well, well, well, the man was learning, she thought. "Will do," she promised.

She noticed he was still standing on the sidewalk, watching her car when she finally turned the corner and drove out of sight. He looked so lonely, she almost went around the block and demanded that he come with her. She could have persuaded him if she'd really tried.

"One step at a time," she murmured to herself. Right now they were frustrating baby steps, two forward, half a dozen back, but after this morning she had a feeling a giant leap forward was just around the corner.

Chapter Eight

For the next few days Maggie was careful not to push too hard. She didn't want to risk the progress she'd made so far. That didn't keep her away from Ryan's Place, though. She turned up most nights, always finding some way to make herself useful. One of these days Ryan would discover he couldn't get along without her.

At the same time, she cleverly avoided any further mention of his accounting system. There was no sense in antagonizing him when they were making such nice advances in other areas. Sooner or later he'd trust her enough to listen to her financial advice. She didn't stop to question why she was so determined to make herself indispensable to a small business when she ought to be out looking for a big corporate position that would make use of her MBA.

In the meantime, there were the books at St. Mary's to be straightened out. Father Francis had none of Ryan's reticence when it came to utilizing Maggie's expertise. In fact, he seemed delighted to have someone take over the task of sorting through the chaotic system the church had been using for decades.

As for the shelter, it had no system at all. If there was a need, donations were found to help. Money came and went in a haphazard manner that would have set an IRS agent's teeth on edge. Maggie didn't doubt for a second that not one cent was spent on anything other than legitimate expenses, but there were few records to prove it.

She stared helplessly at the pile of unorganized receipts that had been crammed into a drawer. "What were you thinking?" she asked Father Francis. "Do you have any idea what kind of dangerous path you've been following? If there was ever an audit . . ." She shuddered just contemplating it.

"It's a bit of a tangle, isn't it?" Father Francis admitted, seemingly not the least big chagrined. "But I don't see the need for a lot of fuss. We've more important things to do. If the money's there, we spend it on those who need our assistance. If it's not, we go out and find what we need. Why complicate things?"

Maggie groaned at his logic. "Have you even filed for nonprofit status?"

"It's an outreach of the church," he said, as if that settled the matter.

"But none of the shelter's funds or activities are on the church's books."

He refused to see the point, clearly trusting that the shelter's mission and good intentions would exempt it from scrutiny.

Maggie tried again. "You might increase the level of giving if people could claim a tax deduction. Instead, you're relying on special collections at the church. Why not reach out to the entire community? Why not build up a solid bank account so there are funds available for an emergency? If you'd had such a fund, you wouldn't have had to turn to Ryan to help with Lamar's surgery. And Ryan could have claimed that money as a deduction on his taxes."

"Ryan doesn't help for the rewards," the priest insisted, his expression set stubbornly.

"I know that," Maggie said, totally exasperated. "But it could be a win-win situation."

"Is that an improvement over an unselfish act of kindness?" the priest asked reasonably.

Maggie sighed. How could she argue with the logic of that? "You won't even consider letting me set up a system?" she asked, then sighed again when he shook his head. "You're turning out to be as impossible as Ryan."

That, apparently, was an accusation he couldn't ignore. Father Francis's sigh was just as deep as Maggie's. "You really think it's important?"

"I do."

"Who's going to take care of all the record keeping it will entail?"

"I will."

For the first time since they'd begun, he beamed. "Well then, if you're promising to take charge, go ahead. The shelter can always use a volunteer." He gave her one of those canny looks that she'd come to consider suspect. "Perhaps you'd like to help a few of the children with their math, while you're here. The math tutor we had recently moved away."

"I didn't offer—" she began, but the priest cut off her protest.

"I know you didn't offer," he conceded. "I'm asking. Your help would be a blessing for the children."

Maggie shook her head at his clever manipulation. "No wonder the shelter hasn't needed a formal fund-raising drive. I'll bet you could single-handedly squeeze money out of Scrooge."

"Actually, it's the Lord who provides," he said with pious innocence. "I just give a gentle nudge here and there to point the way. Will you help the children?"

"When?" Maggie asked, resigned.

"I find after school on Tuesday is good for tutoring. Many of their tests are later in the week. And they haven't yet grown bored with studying, as they have by Thursday or Friday."

"Fine. I'll be here on Tuesdays. I'll come early and work on the books."

He feigned a troubled expression. "That won't interfere with your work, will it? I wouldn't want to interfere with your need to earn a living."

"I'm not working now, as you perfectly well know. Once I do find a job, we'll make whatever adjustments we must."

"You're a good girl, Maggie O'Brien."

"Or an idiot," she murmured.

He grinned at her. "Never that. You've had the good sense to fall in love with Ryan Devaney, haven't you?"

She regarded him with dismay. "Nobody said anything about me falling in love with Ryan."

"Nobody had to. The look is shining in your eyes whenever you're in the same room."

"If that's the case, no wonder he panics when he sees me coming," she said, no longer making any attempt to deny the obvious. She'd fought against putting a label on her feelings, more for Ryan's sake than her own. Maybe it was time she admitted that fascination had turned to something deeper.

The priest patted her hand. "The panic will wear off in time. Ryan's no more a fool than you are. He'll see what's staring him in the face eventually."

"From your lips to God's ear," Maggie said fervently.

Father Francis regarded her serenely. "Aye, child, that's the way of it."

Ryan was beginning to get used to having Maggie turn up at the pub every evening just before suppertime. Sometimes she sat at the bar, blatantly flirting with him. Sometimes she huddled in a booth with Father Francis, scolding him about the church's accounting methods and casting surreptitious glances Ryan's way. And increasingly, whenever it was especially busy, she grabbed an apron off the hook in the kitchen and waited on tables, refusing to accept anything more than whatever tips were left by the customers. Rory and Maureen considered her part of the staff. Juan and Rosita thought she was an angel. As for him, he was still struggling with what to make of her.

"Are you independently wealthy?" Ryan inquired one night a week before Christmas, when she'd turned down his offer of money yet again.

"Hardly, but I have some savings. Besides, this isn't a job," she insisted once again. "I have time on my hands right now, anyway. I enjoy being here. Your customers are the friendliest people I've ever met. And as long as I am here, I may as well pitch in. It's obvious you can use the help."

"I can't deny that," he said.

She looked into his eyes in an expectant way that had his knees going weak and the rest of him going hard.

"If you were to steal a kiss from time to time, it would go a long way toward making it worth my while to be here," she taunted.

The woman could tempt a saint, he thought as she held his gaze. Unable to resist, Ryan tucked an arm around her waist and dragged her close. "Now, that is something I can do," he said, covering her mouth long enough to send a shudder rippling through them both.

It was a risky game they were playing, though. He wanted so much more. His yearning for her had deepened each day, until every minute was a struggle not to haul her up to his apartment.

He'd vowed, though, that he wouldn't let her tempt him into making a mistake they'd both regret. No matter how she got under his skin, he was going to be the sensible one and keep his hands to himself. Still, he couldn't help wondering what it would be like to strip away those thick, soft sweaters she wore, to peel away her skintight jeans and the lacy panties he fantasized about, and bury himself deep inside her. He hadn't wanted to experience that kind of closeness with a woman—real intimacy that went beyond sex—in a long time, if ever.

Instead, he settled for the occasional kiss, deliberately keeping them brief enough to permit him to cling to sanity. For once in his life, he was trying to do the right thing.

Not that Maggie did anything to help. She had absolutely no reservations about using her own hands to torment him. She was always skimming a caress across his knuckles, patting his cheek and on one especially memorable occasion, linking her fingers through his and pressing an impulsive kiss on their joined hands, while gazing deeply into his eyes in a way that had him losing track of everything, including his own name. Oh, yes, Miss Maggie was a toucher, and it was driving him flat-out crazy.

Father Francis clearly found the whole situation highly amusing. Whenever he thought Ryan might not be tormented enough, he drew Ryan's attention back to Maggie with one observation or another meant to remind him of just how desirable she was. The priest had turned into a determined matchmaker, who had absolutely no shame about the methods he used. Rory was just as bad. And even Maggie's family seemed to have bestowed their approval on the match, turning up singly or a few at a time to sit at the bar or in a booth. They seemed to have adopted Ryan as one of them without waiting for the link between him and Maggie to be formalized.

With so many people giving their blessing, Ryan might even have been tempted to get involved in a fling with Maggie-of-the-roving-hands . . . if she'd been another kind of woman. But Maggie was all about happily-ever-after. One look at her family was evidence enough of that.

Unfortunately, Ryan knew better than anyone that there was no such thing. Someday a man would let her down and she'd know the truth, but it wasn't going to be him.

Besides, he couldn't help thinking that she'd adopted him as she might a bedraggled kitten she pitied. One day she'd tire of him and move along to a man whose heart wasn't cast in stone. Since abandonment had been a sore subject with him for some years now, he didn't intend to risk it a second time.

None of that kept him from his yearning, though. Right now, she was across the room, chatting with a customer, her auburn hair flowing to her shoulders in shiny waves, her face devoid of any makeup beyond a touch of pale lipstick, and beautiful just the same. Ryan stared at her and barely managed to contain a sigh.

"You wouldn't be so frustrated, lad, if you'd make a move on the lady," Rory observed.

"You've hit on the problem," Ryan responded, his gaze not shifting away from Maggie. "She's a *lady.*"

"But I think you'd find her more than willing."

Ryan didn't doubt it. In fact, there were so many signals and unspoken invitations sizzling in the air, it was a wonder half his customers didn't wind up singed. "That's not the point," he said testily.

"There won't be any rewards for saintliness in this instance," Rory said.

"I'm not looking for rewards. I'm trying to be sensible. I have nothing to offer a woman like Maggie."

"She seems to think otherwise."

"Because she doesn't know me that well," Ryan said. She didn't know that he had no heart, no love at all to give. Quite likely, even with what she did know, she'd dismissed the possibility that he would never allow himself to fall in love, would never marry and risk disappointing a family as his parents had disappointed him. She was deluding herself, because she wanted to believe the best of him.

"Again, I say she thinks otherwise," Rory said. "She seems to know all she needs to."

"Then it's up to me to protect her from herself."

"She won't thank you. Women seldom appreciate a man doing their thinking for them."

Ryan gave him a rueful look. "It's not her thanks I'm after. A man protects a woman he cares about because it's the right thing to do."

"We're back to that bloody try for sainthood again," Rory chided. "You're a mere mortal, Ryan. Why not act like one?"

"Is that what you do? Is that why any woman who crosses the threshold in here is fair game to you?"

"Whatever happens between me and any woman is a mutual decision," Rory countered. "That's because I think of them as equals and respect that they know their own minds. Perhaps you should give Maggie some credit for knowing hers."

There was sense to what Rory said. Ryan could admit that, but he couldn't dwell on it. If he did, the game would be lost. He and Maggie would have their momentary pleasure, but the regrets would pour in on its heels.

No, his way was better . . . even if he was having the devil's own time remembering why.

Lamar's surgery was scheduled for Friday morning. As of midnight on Thursday, Jack Reilly had had absolutely no luck in finding the boy's father. Ryan decided he was going to have to take matters into his own hands. If there was even a chance that Monroe was anywhere around the Boston harbor, he was going to find him before that boy went into the operating room in the morning.

"You can't be serious," Jack said when Ryan asked him to describe every single place he'd already searched. "If I haven't found him, he's not there."

"I refuse to accept that," Ryan said, aware that Maggie had joined them and was blatantly eavesdropping. "Now, are you going to tell me and save me some time, or do I have to spend the entire night covering ground you've already covered?"

Jack sighed. "Never mind. I'll come with you. Maybe we'll get lucky."

"I'm coming, too," Maggie announced, running to grab her coat and purse.

Ryan stopped her in her tracks, frowning at

her. “It’s late. You have no business wandering around down there at this hour.”

“You’re going, aren’t you?” She scowled right back at him. “And if you point out that you’re a man, I’m going to have to dump a pitcher of ale over your head.” She was already reaching for it to emphasize the point.

“Maggie,” Ryan protested, then sighed in the face of her determined expression and her firm grip on the pitcher. “Okay then, let’s go. We don’t have the time to waste arguing.”

“Such a gracious capitulation,” she noted as she set the pitcher back on the bar and swept past him.

Jack gave him a pitying look. “She’s a woman with a mind of her own, isn’t she?”

“Tell me about it,” Ryan said dryly.

Together, the three of them combed the bars along the waterfront. They spoke to fishermen and dockworkers as they began to arrive for work in the predawn hours. When people seemed reluctant to talk to them, Maggie stepped in and charmed them into opening up. Despite her best efforts, though, no one recalled a man fitting Jamal Monroe’s description.

“Dammit, that boy cannot go into surgery thinking that his own father doesn’t care enough to be there,” Ryan said when they’d retreated to a small, crowded café filled with the raucous banter of men who spent their lives on the water.

He cupped his hands around a mug of strong coffee, grateful for the warmth after being out for hours in the damp, cold air.

"We're going to make sure that doesn't happen," Maggie soothed with unwavering confidence.

Suddenly a shadow fell over the table. Ryan glanced up into chocolate-brown eyes that glinted with anger and suspicion. The man was dressed warmly, in worn yet clean clothes, but he was too thin. And undeniable exhaustion and strain were evident on his dark face.

"I hear you've been asking a lot of questions about Jamal Monroe," he said. "Why?"

Ryan suspected that this was Lamar's father, though the man hadn't admitted it outright. He gestured toward the fourth chair at their table. "Join us. How about a cup of coffee and some breakfast?"

The man hesitated, but the lure of the hot drink and food apparently won him over. With a respectful nod toward Maggie, he sat down, though he kept his jacket on as if he wanted to be ready to take off at once if the need arose.

Ryan didn't say anything until the waitress had brought coffee and taken the man's order. Then he looked him directly in the eye. "We've been bumping up against a brick wall for hours now. I don't suppose you have any idea how we can find Monroe?"

"Could be," the man said cautiously. "But you

still haven't said why you're so anxious to find him. You friends of his?"

"No, we've never met," Ryan admitted, keeping his gaze locked on the man's face. "It's about his son, Lamar."

There was a definite flicker of recognition, maybe even something else. Fear, perhaps.

"You know his boy?" the man asked.

Ryan nodded. "And his wife. They've been staying at the St. Mary's homeless shelter."

This time there was no mistaking the reaction. "Why are they there?" he asked with more emotion in his voice. "They had a halfway decent apartment when I—" He looked flustered at the telling slip and hurriedly corrected it. "When *he* left."

At Ryan's nod, it was Maggie who continued, her tone gentle. "They needed help. Without Mr. Monroe at home, they couldn't make it. And Lamar needs surgery, but once Mr. Monroe quit his job, their insurance was cut off."

The man's shoulders slumped, and his eyes filled with tears. "Damn, I never meant it to come to that," he said, his voice thick. "I thought I'd be back in time to make things right. I just needed some time away to think."

Ryan and Jack exchanged a look.

"Then you are Jamal," Ryan said gently.

He nodded. "Even if I am a sorry excuse for a husband and a father, I love those two."

"Then why did you take off?" Ryan asked, barely managing to keep an accusatory note out of his voice.

"If you know about the surgery, then you probably know Lamar's medical condition is hereditary. He got it from me," Jamal said, his tone filled with guilt.

"Through no fault of your own," Maggie insisted fiercely, resting her hand on his. "You didn't know you had the problem, so how could you know you could pass it along to your son? Nobody is blaming you."

"I blame myself," Jamal said heatedly, " 'cause the honest truth is, I did know. Soon as that doctor started talking, I remembered the problems I had when I was a kid."

"You had a heart problem that required surgery?" Ryan asked, stunned.

Jamal nodded. "I was younger than Lamar is now, and I spent a lot of time in the hospital. My folks never explained much about what was going on, and I was too little to understand if they had. I wasn't even in school yet, so I must have been three, maybe four years old. Once I had the surgery, I could do anything I wanted. Didn't take me long to put all of the bad times out of my head. Years go by, and it's like it happened to some other person, if you remember at all. Never crossed my mind that I could pass it along to a child of mine."

"That's perfectly normal," Maggie reassured him, shooting a warning look at Ryan. "People don't always consider all the genetic ramifications before having kids. They fall in love, get married and start a family. Unless they've had to confront a congenital illness all their lives, it's the last thing on their minds. Letitia doesn't blame you for Lamar being sick. Lamar certainly doesn't blame you. If they don't, how can you go on blaming yourself? And it's time to forgive yourself, too, for being human and running out. The important thing is to be there for Lamar now."

Jamal shook his head. "Letitia's bound to be fit to be tied. That woman has a temper when she's riled, and she has every right to be furious with me. She probably won't let me anywhere near the boy."

"You're wrong," Ryan said. "The only thing on her mind now is what's best for Lamar, and he needs to see his daddy before he goes into surgery."

Jamal seemed startled. "Thought you said he couldn't have it, because they lost their insurance."

Ryan carefully avoided Maggie's gaze. "The shelter was able to help," he explained. "The surgery's this morning. If you're willing, we can take you to see him. I know if I were a father, there's nowhere else I'd be today."

Maggie gave Jamal's hand a squeeze. "Please.

Lamar needs you. He's scared. Having you there will go a long way toward reassuring him that everything's going to turn out all right, especially once you tell him that you had the same surgery a long time ago."

Jamal seemed to struggle with himself, but he finally nodded and pushed back from the table. "Take me to see my boy."

Ryan paid the check and led the way back to the car. It was still early enough that they didn't get tangled up in rush hour as they made their way to the children's hospital where Lamar's surgery was scheduled for eight o'clock. He pulled up at the front entrance.

"Maggie, why don't you take him to Lamar's room while I park the car? I'll be up in a few minutes."

She regarded him with a penetrating look. "You are coming in, though, aren't you? Lamar will want to see you, too."

"I'll be there," he said, overcoming his reluctance to give her the answer she was all but demanding.

She bent down to whisper in his ear. "Five minutes, Devaney. If you're not there, I'm going to come looking for you."

Ryan didn't doubt for a second that she would do just that. "I gave you my word," he said.

"And promises mean as much to you as they do to me?" she asked.

He gazed into her eyes. "I don't make them unless I mean to keep them. If anyone knows the devastation of broken promises, it's me."

She rested her hand against his cheek. "I'll see you inside, then."

Ryan watched her walk away with Jamal.

"She's a remarkable woman, isn't she?" Jack noted.

"Yeah, she certainly is."

"If I were you, I wouldn't let her get away."

Ryan scowled. "Not you, too," he protested. "Geez, if I get any more matchmaking advice from people who hang out at the pub, I'll have to turn the place into a lonely-hearts club."

"Not a bad idea," Jack said. "And if there are any more out there like Maggie, send 'em my way." He reached for his door handle. "I think I'll catch a cab and head for home."

"You're not going to stick around to make sure I go inside?" Ryan inquired. "I thought maybe you'd nominate yourself to see to it I don't let Maggie down."

"If you let her down, you're an idiot," Jack said succinctly. "And frankly, if you're that dumb, I don't want to know about it. Right now I'm feeling all warm and fuzzy toward you for helping Lamar."

Ryan laughed. "Go. I'll give you a call once he's out of surgery."

Jack nodded. "You do that." He grinned. "Or

give Maggie the honor. I wouldn't mind waking up to the sound of her voice in my ear."

"Go to hell," Ryan said. If Maggie was going to be whispering in any man's ear, it was going to be his. And it was looking more and more as if that was going to be inevitable.

Chapter Nine

Maggie knew precisely why Ryan had let her be the one to escort Mr. Monroe into the hospital to see his son. He hadn't wanted to be a part of an emotional family reunion, even if he was the one responsible for making it happen. Because there had been no reunion for him and his brothers, the prospect of this one made him uncomfortable.

He needed to be there, though. He needed to put his discomfort aside if he was ever to know that happy endings were possible.

As Maggie and Jamal Monroe stepped off the elevator, she turned and looked at him. "I know I have no right to ask this, especially after insisting that you get right over here, but would you mind waiting a few more minutes before you see Lamar?"

He regarded her with surprise. "You want to go in and make sure they want to see me?"

"No, I know how happy they'll be that you're here. In fact, that's the point."

He studied her knowingly. "This has something to do with Mr. Devaney, doesn't it? You seemed real anxious that he not take off. You still worried he might not show up?"

"No, I'm sure he'll be here any second, and I think he should be a part of this."

"So he gets the credit he's due for tracking me down?"

She smiled at the all-too-cynical reaction. "No, so he can see for himself the look in Lamar's eyes when you walk through the door."

At her explanation, his natural suspicion gave way. He nodded in apparent understanding. "I suppose a couple more minutes won't make any difference," he said. "And I do owe the man for his trouble."

"He doesn't want your thanks or your sense of obligation," Maggie was quick to assure him. "He just wants you and your son to be together. I can't explain why this meeting is so important to him, but it is. Trust me."

They were still standing by the elevator when Letitia Monroe emerged from Lamar's room and spotted them. An entire spectrum of emotions flashed across her face, from anger to love to relief. Her husband took a few hesitant steps in her direction, then paused and waited. She hurried down the corridor and straight into his arms. Her shoulders shook with sobs as he tried ineffectively to console her.

"Jamal Monroe, I ought to slap you silly for putting us through all this worry," Letitia said finally, sniffing loudly and wiping her eyes with a tissue Maggie provided. "But I'm too relieved to see you. The rest will have to wait." She glanced around. "Where's Mr. Devaney? I know he had something to do with you being here."

The elevator doors whooshed open just then, and Ryan emerged. Letitia threw her arms around him in a fierce hug that almost knocked him off his feet.

"I will be indebted to you for the rest of my life," she declared. "Thank you for finding Jamal and getting him here in time."

"The truth is, he found us," Ryan said modestly. "All I did was poke around and ask a few questions."

"But I don't doubt for a minute that it was all that poking around that stirred things up and flushed him out," she said with conviction. She slipped her hand into her husband's. "Let's go see our boy."

They started down the hall, but Ryan held back. Maggie regarded him with a questioning look, but it was Letitia who turned around and said impatiently, "Hurry up. Lamar's expecting you. And I imagine Father Francis has heard about all of the boy's pitiful jokes he can stand for one morning."

"I shouldn't intrude," Ryan said, looking around desperately for someplace to flee.

"Intrude, nothing. You're part of this family till the end of time," Letitia said emphatically. "And I don't want to hear anyone saying otherwise, including you."

Maggie grinned at the woman's belief that she had the right to boss Ryan around. Maybe she should steal a page out of Letitia's book. Ryan appeared a little shell-shocked.

"I guess she told *you,*" Maggie teased.

Ryan seemed a little bewildered at being summarily made a part of the Monroe family, but he snagged Maggie's hand and followed Letitia.

"You know," Maggie began casually. "It's an interesting thing about families."

He regarded her warily. "Oh?"

"Some people spend a lifetime surrounded by blood relatives they don't get along with much. Some have wonderful families like mine." She gave him a pointed look. "And some get to choose the people they consider family."

He gave her a wry smile. "I get it, Maggie."

"I hope so," she said softly. "I really do." She figured their future depended on it.

Ryan hesitated again once they reached Lamar's room. Despite Letitia's insistence that he belonged there, he felt like an interloper at what should be a very private moment. But even if he'd wanted to hang back, there was Maggie watching him with that beseeching, hopeful expression. He couldn't let her down. And he wasn't too keen on being the recipient of one of Father Francis's disappointed looks, either, to say nothing of another outburst of Letitia's temper.

"You go in first," Letitia instructed. "Tell my baby you have a surprise for him."

"Me? Shouldn't you be doing that?"

She glanced at Maggie, then regarded him with a steady look. "Something tells me it's important that you do it."

Recognizing that he was defeated, Ryan sucked in a sharp breath, then walked into the room. His nervousness eased the instant he saw Lamar's face light up. Father Francis smiled at him and stepped aside to give Ryan room at the boy's bedside.

"You came!" Lamar said. "Mom said you would, but it was getting late. They've already given me some kinda shot. I'm getting real sleepy."

Ryan rubbed his knuckles over the boy's head. "Don't go to sleep just yet. I have a surprise, and you're going to want to be wide awake for it."

Lamar's eyes widened. "A surprise? For me? What is it?"

Ryan nodded toward the door. "Look over there."

Just as he said it, Jamal stepped into the room.

"Dad," Lamar whispered, reaching for Ryan's hand and gazing up at him with a grateful expression. "You found my dad. I knew you would."

As Jamal reached the side of the bed, his eyes filled with tears. "Hi, son. I'm sorry for worrying you, for letting you and your mom go through all of this alone."

"It's okay, Dad. I knew you'd come back. I just knew it."

Jamal bent down, his tears spilling onto his son's face as he hugged him. "I love you, boy. Don't you ever forget that. And once you've had this surgery and are good as new again, you and I are gonna do all the things we've always talked about. That's a promise."

Lamar looked at Ryan, his eyes shining. "And my dad never breaks his promises. Not ever." He glanced toward his mother. "Ain't that right, Mom?"

"*Isn't* it, right," Letitia corrected. Wisely, she didn't mention the promise Jamal had made to her to be there in sickness and in health, in good times and bad. "Your daddy's here now. That's all that matters."

Just then the nurse came into the room with an orderly. "Time to go, Lamar."

He clung to his father's hand. "You'll be here after the operation, right? You're not going to go away again?"

"I'll be right by your side when you wake up," Jamal assured him.

The next few hours passed in a blur of lousy coffee, tasteless food and pacing. There were a dozen times when Ryan would have made an excuse and escaped, but one glance at Maggie kept him right where he was. From the moment they'd met, she'd seemed to expect the best from him, the same as Father Francis. Now there were two people in his life Ryan hoped never to disappoint. He was surprised he didn't feel more pressured by it, but the truth was, it felt good to know there were people counting on him and that, so far at least, he had never let them down.

Across the room Letitia and Jamal sat side by side, hand in hand, drawing comfort from each other the way they should have all these weeks.

"Looks like Letitia has forgiven him already," he said to Maggie, unable to keep the surprise out of his voice.

"Human beings make mistakes," Maggie said quietly. "Wise human beings understand that and forgive them."

"How the hell do you forgive someone for walking out when he's needed the most?" Ryan demanded, his chin jutting forward.

Maggie regarded him with a penetrating look. "Are we talking about Jamal now, or your parents?"

Ryan ground his teeth. "Jamal, of course," he said tightly.

"Ryan—"

"Don't," he said, shooting to his feet and walking away from the lecture so evidently on the tip of her tongue. He didn't need anyone, not even Maggie, telling him that there could be any possible justification for what his parents had done to him and his brothers. He certainly wasn't going to entertain the notion of forgiving them for dumping three boys into the foster care system before taking off to who-knew-where.

He moved to the window and stared outside, only halfway aware that snow was falling, leaving a coating of white on the ground. Christmas was fast approaching, and it was his second most hated holiday of the year, right after Thanksgiving. He never failed to spend the day trying to imagine where his brothers might be, what they might have endured. If their holidays had been anything like his, they must hate the season, as well.

"I take it Maggie dared to say something about your parents," Father Francis said, coming to stand beside him.

"What makes you think that?" Ryan asked.

"Little else puts such a scowl on your face," the priest replied. "Besides, it's natural for you to think of them on a day like this. Seeing Lamar reunited with his father must make you wonder a little about your own father."

"I am not thinking of my parents," Ryan insisted. "Or at least I wasn't until the two of you decided to pester me about them."

Father Francis waited until Ryan eventually turned to face him, then said, "Are you going to allow two people you claim to have no feelings for, at all, control the way you live the rest of your life?"

"What the devil are you talking about? They control nothing!" Ryan declared.

"Oh, really? Have you given one second's thought to a future with Maggie?" The priest held up a silencing hand when Ryan would have responded. "And don't waste your breath telling me you're not attracted to her, because anyone with eyes can see that you are. Yet you do nothing about it, because in your heart you know it would have to lead somewhere, to a place you won't allow yourself to go."

"Shouldn't you be praying for Lamar, instead of giving me advice on my love life?" he inquired sourly.

"I'm a modern man. I've learned to multitask," Father Francis said.

Despite his irritation, Ryan bit back a laugh. "And who taught you that term? Maggie, I imagine."

"The girl's an inspiration, to be sure," Father Francis said cheerfully. "But then, even you can see that, can't you?"

Ryan sighed as the priest retreated to sit with Letitia and Jamal, apparently satisfied that he'd gotten his message across. Ryan glanced over at Maggie, saw the worry in her eyes as she watched the door, then the lingering flicker of hurt when she caught him staring at her. Resigned, he went back to her side.

"I'm sorry for snapping your head off before,"

he said. "And I'm sorry I keep doing things that necessitate so many apologies."

"It's okay," she said with another display of that ready forgiveness she seemed willing to dispense, no matter how unreasonable he'd been. "We're all under a lot of stress this morning."

"That's no excuse." He noted the dark circles under her eyes, the strain around her mouth. "Maggie, you must be exhausted. Why not let me drive you home?"

She shook her head. "Not until we hear something."

"Okay then, at least rest for a bit." He sat beside her and slipped an arm around her shoulders, giving her a gentle tug. After a moment's resistance, she gingerly put her head on his shoulder. "That's better. Now close your eyes. If the doctor comes, I promise I'll wake you."

She didn't respond, and moments later he felt the tension in her shoulders ease. Soon after, her breathing deepened, and something inside him eased, as well. He had only the dimmest memory of feeling this protective toward anyone, quite likely because he hadn't wanted to remember that, when it was truly important, he hadn't been able to protect his brothers from the worst hurt of all.

Maggie couldn't recall when she'd ever felt so safe. In her dream, she was in a house that was being buffeted by a powerful northeast wind, but she was safe and warm, tucked in Ryan's arms in front of a cozy fire. She had the sense that as long as she was in his embrace, nothing could ever harm her.

She shifted sleepily, cuddling closer to all that strength and heat, only to hear his voice whispering urgently in her ear.

"Come on, Maggie. Wake up, darlin'. The doctor's here."

It was the last, more than the term of endearment, that penetrated. Her eyes snapped open, and she immediately spotted the surgeon in his operating room attire standing beside Letitia and Jamal. Her gaze shot to Ryan.

"Have you heard what he's saying? Is it good news?"

"I can't hear from here."

"What about his expression? How did he look?"

Ryan regarded her blankly.

"Was he happy? Sad? What?" she prodded. "You read people's moods every single night at the pub. Can't you read his?"

"Maggie, we could find out everything if we went over there," he suggested with exaggerated patience.

"I don't want to intrude."

"Look at it this way—if the news is good, they'd want us to share in it," he said. "If it's bad, they're going to need our support."

She blinked at that, struck by the fact that a man who professed no emotional entanglements could still have the most amazingly sensitive insights. He should give himself credit for them more often. "Of course you're right." She stood up and grabbed his hand, pulling him along with her.

As they reached the small gathering, Letitia turned to them, her eyes brimming with tears. Maggie's heart stopped. "Oh, no," she whispered, her hand tightening around Ryan's.

"No, no," Letitia said, gathering her into a hug. "It's good news. He's going to be fine. My boy's going to be fine." She turned to Ryan, hugging him, as well. "And it's all because of you, not just because you paid for the surgery, but because you got his daddy here. That gave Lamar the will to live. I know it did."

"Now, it's still going to be a critical twenty-four to forty-eight hours," the doctor cautioned. "But I have every reason to believe Lamar will come through this with flying colors."

"It's a miracle, that's what it is," Letitia declared, her cheeks damp.

"It is, indeed," Jamal said. He turned to Ryan. "Thank you."

"I'm glad I was able to help," Ryan said, clearly uncomfortable with their gratitude. "And now that we know Lamar's made it through the surgery, I'm going to get Maggie home. She was out with me most of the night trying to find you, Jamal. She's beat."

"I'll come by later, though," Maggie promised, too tired to waste any breath on a futile argument. "And if you need anything, anything at all, you call me." She pressed a slip of paper into Letitia's hands.

"Bless you, girl. You, too, Mr. Devaney."

Outside in the crisp air, Maggie drew in a deep breath, then turned to Ryan. "I can't begin to tell you how relieved I am. You must be, too. And if we are, just imagine what Letitia and Jamal must be feeling."

"They love their son. Of course they're relieved," Ryan said.

Maggie regarded him intently. "You know, Ryan, it's possible that your parents did what they did because they loved you and your brothers."

"Don't be absurd."

"How will you ever know if you don't try to find them and make them explain?"

"Why the hell would I ever want to see them again?"

"So you can put the past to rest."

"If you knew the whole story, you'd never suggest such a thing," he said fiercely.

"Then tell me."

He sighed, a lost, lonely expression on his face. "Maybe one of these days I will."

"Why not now?" she pushed.

"Because we're both exhausted."

"Buy me a strong cup of coffee and I can listen."

He smiled wearily at that. "Trying to get me when my defenses are down?"

"Absolutely," she said without hesitation.

He leaned down and covered her mouth with his. The kiss was sweet and all too brief. "Ah, Maggie, what am I going to do with you?"

"Are you seriously asking for suggestions?" she teased.

His gaze captured hers and held, amusement darkening into desire, then giving way to regret. "Maybe one of these days," he said.

She bit back her own regrets. "I'll hold you to that, Ryan Devaney."

He laughed. "I don't doubt that for a second. In fact, I'm fairly certain you have a whole list of things I'm expected to make good on."

"None you can't handle," she said with confidence.

Chapter Ten

Ryan had absolutely no intention of allowing Maggie to drive all the way home in her current state of exhaustion. Since he wasn't one bit better off, there was only one answer: she'd have to stay at his place. Proposing that, while making it clear it was an innocent suggestion, was going to be a neat trick.

He pulled to a stop in a parking space down the block from the pub and glanced over at her. She was struggling to keep her eyes open. He left the car and circled to open the passenger door.

"Okay, come with me," he said, his tone firm.

"My car's right across the street," she said, when he steered her toward the pub.

"And if you get behind the wheel and drive as far as the corner, you're likely to fall asleep and crash into something. I won't have that on my conscience."

She tilted her head and regarded him curiously. "Then what are you suggesting?"

"You'll sleep at my place," he said, trying to be grimly matter-of-fact about it.

"How intriguing!" A smile tugged at her lips. "Just minutes ago you vetoed that idea."

Ryan laughed at her typically give-an-inch-take-a-mile response. "No, that is not what I vetoed. You'll be sleeping in the bed. I'll be on the sofa."

A glint of amusement lit her eyes. "Now, where's the fun in that, Ryan Devaney?"

He managed a severe expression. "Don't you be tempting me, Maggie O'Brien. What would your fine father and brothers think of that?"

"They have nothing to do with my personal life," she assured him airily.

"Do they know that?" he inquired with skepticism.

She sighed heavily. "Probably not."

"Then perhaps we'd best do this my way for now," he said as he led the way upstairs to his apartment over the pub.

When he walked through the doorway, he tried to view the room through Maggie's eyes. The windows across the front let in a lot of light and the bare wood floors gleamed softly, but beyond a sofa, a comfortable chair and the television that he never bothered to flip on, there wasn't much to recommend it.

To the left, the kitchen had new appliances he'd used no more than a handful of times because he took most of his meals downstairs in the pub. Even his coffeemaker was in like-new condition.

"The minimalist style, I see," Maggie observed, still standing in the entry. "I imagine most people think they get a better sense of you from the pub downstairs."

Her thoughtful comment made him wary. "And you don't?"

"No, I think this gives away more. No clutter. No personal objects to give any hint about the man you are. All your secrets are protected here." She met his gaze. "Is the bedroom any better?"

"Not if you're looking to unravel any secrets," he said with an edge of defensiveness.

He showed her the way, then stood back as she surveyed the king-size bed with its dark-green quilt tossed haphazardly over sheets in a paler shade of green, the oak dresser with nothing beyond a pile of loose change on top, the digital clock on the bedside stand and an antique rocker in the corner. She blinked when her gaze fell on that, then turned to him, her face alight with curiosity.

"A family heirloom?" she asked, crossing over to rub her hand over the oak wood with its soft sheen.

"Hardly."

"You're fond of antiques, then?"

"Not especially," he said, the defensiveness back in his voice. He should never have brought her here. He could see that now. She liked digging beneath the surface of things to the raw truths beneath.

"Back problems?" she persisted unrelentingly.

"No, and what does that have to do with having a rocker in my room?"

"They say President Kennedy had a rocker because of chronic back problems. I've seen pictures of it."

Ryan nodded. "Okay, yes, I guess I have heard something about that, but it's got nothing to do with this. I saw it in a shop and I liked it. End of story."

Her gaze narrowed with obvious disbelief. "Did your mother rock you when you were little?"

Ryan bit back a curse at the accurate guess. "How the hell would I remember a thing like that?" he asked derisively.

Maggie's gaze never left his face. "She did, didn't she? That's why you bought this chair. It reminds you of one your family had."

The truth was, he suspected it might have been *this* chair. On the one occasion he'd ventured back to his childhood neighborhood, he'd found the rocker in a shop not all that far from where they'd lived. He'd been drawn to it at once, and despite his claim that he wanted nothing at all to do with the past, he hadn't been able to put it out of his mind. He'd gone back the next day and bought the rocker, but only after asking the shop owner what he knew about the original owner. Unfortunately, the man had bought the shop from someone else, and the rocker had been a part of the inventory. He'd known nothing at all about its history, not even the year in which it had been purchased.

"Maggie, drop it, okay? It's just a chair."

"And if someone were to take an ax to it, it wouldn't bother you at all?" she inquired innocently.

Hands jammed in his pockets, he shrugged. "It would be a waste of a beautiful piece of craftsmanship, nothing more," he asserted.

She sighed at his response. "If you insist."

"I do." He gestured toward a door across the hall. "The bathroom's over there. There are towels in the closet. If you need anything else, let me know."

"Just a phone. I need to call home and let them know what's going on."

He felt guilty for not having suggested it right away. "Given the way they worry, they must be frantic by now."

She shook her head. "I doubt it. I called them last night and told them I was going to be with you."

Ryan couldn't have been more stunned if she'd punched him in the gut. "You told them that? In those words?"

She grinned at his discomfort. "Maybe not those precise words, but that was the gist of it, yes."

Curious despite himself, he asked, "How did they react?"

"Mother said I need to bring you home to dinner tonight."

"That's it?"

"Oh, I imagine she'll have quite a bit to say when you get there, but last night that's all she said," Maggie replied, clearly enjoying herself.

"Then let's postpone that dinner for a while—like maybe ten years from now."

She laughed. "If you think that will work, you don't know my mother at all. She's counting on tonight. No excuses accepted."

"You'll just have to extend my apologies," Ryan insisted. "Tonight's out of the question."

"A prior engagement?"

"Nope. Just a healthy desire to live."

"I don't think it will come to that," Maggie said soothingly. "My folks haven't killed a prospective son-in-law yet. And before you panic—which, by the way, I can see that you're doing—you should know that they regard any male of an appropriate age as prospective marriage material. It's not as if they're getting invitations printed as we speak."

"I should hope not," he said fervently.

She frowned at him. "You know, if I were a less confident woman, I might be offended."

"Maggie, you know where I stand on this. I don't do commitment. I don't do love."

"So you've mentioned."

She didn't seem particularly dismayed. Either she didn't care or she didn't believe him. "It's not something you should forget," he told her, to make the point clearer.

"As if you're likely to let me," she scoffed.

Ryan still wasn't at all convinced she was taking him seriously. However, prolonging the subject struck him as a decidedly lousy idea. "Get some sleep," he muttered, then left the room and closed the door behind him.

The woman was dangerous. As if she couldn't tempt him with a glance, now she was deliberately taunting him every chance she got. One of these days, his willpower was going to snap and his common sense was going to fly right out the window, and then nothing would keep him from joining her in that bed of his. In fact, right now, with the image of her snuggled beneath his sheets firmly implanted in his brain, it was almost more than he could cope with.

Just to be sure he didn't give in to the desire swirling through him, he left the apartment and locked the door securely behind him. Of course, short of his tossing the key in the river, there was nothing to prevent him from unlocking the door and going right back in there an hour from now and struggling with the same neediness. To prevent any chance of that, he went downstairs in search of coffee and Rory's company.

The cook glanced up when he walked in. "I thought I heard you moving about upstairs," he said, and gestured toward a pot of coffee. "The coffee's fresh and strong."

"Thanks," Ryan said, pouring himself a cup.

Rory gave him a sly look. "Of course, I also thought I heard another set of footsteps and a lovely feminine voice. Those wouldn't belong to our Maggie, would they? Have you finally come to your senses where she's concerned?"

"I never lost my senses, which is why I'm down here and she's up there," Ryan retorted.

Rory regarded him with disappointment. "You're breaking my heart, lad. You're a disgrace to all the males of Ireland."

Ryan thought of what Maggie was offering him, of everything he was fighting so hard to resist. He weighed that against a lifetime of noble restraint that had earned him nothing but loneliness. He sighed heavily.

"It's entirely possible that you're right," Ryan conceded.

"Then do something about it."

That image of a naked Maggie sliding beneath his sheets slammed into Ryan's head again. It was getting harder and harder to remember why he needed to resist.

"One of these days, maybe I will," he said, a note of wistfulness creeping into his voice.

"No time like the present," Rory reminded him.

Ryan shook his head. "Some things can't be rushed."

"Would Maggie view you coming back upstairs as rushing her?"

"No," he admitted ruefully. "I'm the one who's

slowed the pace of things. I can't afford a mistake."

"What sort of mistake?" Rory asked, clearly bewildered.

Ryan didn't answer. How could he explain to a man who made a habit of loving and leaving women that once Ryan allowed Maggie to touch him, she'd be a part of his soul?

And that would give her the power to destroy him if she were ever to walk away.

Maggie was relieved to hear the answering machine when she called home to let her family know the outcome of Lamar's surgery and to tell them she was still in town. She wasn't quite ready to try to explain Ryan's continued reticence to come to dinner. Knowing her mother, Maggie suspected Nell wasn't going to take the refusal lightly. When it came to self-proclaimed missions, Nell O'Brien was even quicker to rush in than her daughter. Maggie had a feeling that would be more pressure than Ryan could handle.

She thought of his reaction to her guess that the rocker had reminded him of his mother. He'd obviously been dismayed that she'd hit on the truth. Clearly he didn't like the fact that she was chipping away at that protective wall he'd erected around himself and could see into his heart. Maggie recognized that she needed to be careful, especially since her preference would be to take a sledgehammer to what was left of that wall. Rather than poking and prodding about the Devaneys, she was going to fill Ryan's head with stories of the O'Briens until he grew comfortable with the idea of *her* family, even if he couldn't deal with his own.

Sighing, she snuggled more securely around the pillow that still held Ryan's faint, masculine scent. For now, this was the only way she was likely to get close to him, but that would change eventually. Maggie could be patient when she had to be . . . especially now that she thought she knew how to break down that wall.

It was afternoon when she woke. Sun was streaming in the bedroom window. Maggie yawned and stretched, then listened for some sound to indicate that Ryan had returned to the apartment. All she heard were street sounds and the distant clatter of pots and pans, coming no doubt from the pub kitchen downstairs.

Wrapping herself in one of Ryan's shirts that she found hanging on the back of the door, she slipped across the hall to the bathroom and showered, then dressed. Using his hair dryer, she did what she could to coax some waves into her hair, then ventured downstairs, where she found the pub empty.

The sound of voices in the kitchen drew her. Poking her head around the door, she scanned the room for Ryan, but saw no sign of him. Rory, however, was chopping the vegetables for Irish stew, while Rosita sat nearby, her feet up.

"Taking a break?" Maggie asked with a grin.

"Señor Rory not let me help," Rosita responded, sounding thoroughly disgusted. "I can chop, *sí?* That is not so difficult."

"You need to stay off your feet," Rory countered.

Rosita rolled her eyes. "He is worse than Juan."

"Does Ryan realize he's paying her to rest?" Maggie inquired.

"I'm in charge of the kitchen," Rory claimed defensively. "I see no need to tell himself how I'm running it or who's doing what. As long as there's food for the customers, he's got no cause to complain."

Maggie chuckled. "You're an angel, Rory."

"You'd best be keeping that to yourself, Maggie. I have a reputation as a tyrant to protect."

"Don't worry. I won't give away your secret. Where *is* your boss, by the way?"

"In the pub."

"I didn't see him."

"Check the booth in the back corner. He was asleep on the bench last time I checked."

"Why on earth would he sleep down here when there was a perfectly good sofa upstairs?" she asked. "To say nothing of half a bed."

Rory's eyes sparkled with amusement. "Now

that's a question you should be asking him, but I think you can figure it out if you put your mind to it."

"It's because I was in the other half of that bed, wasn't it?" she asked, astonished that her presence had actually scared the man out of his own home.

"You never heard me say such a thing, now did you?" Rory replied, a grin splitting his face.

"He doesn't trust himself around me," she concluded with a sense of wonder. She'd suspected it, but the confirmation was music to her ears.

"That would be my impression," Rory agreed. He studied her intently. "What do you intend to do about this power you have over him?"

Rather than replying, she met his gaze. "Any suggestions?"

"Now if a woman affected me the way you affect our Ryan, I wouldn't mind if she were to make an outright pass at me," the Irish cook said, then sighed heavily. "But sadly, Ryan is a better man than I. I think a subtler approach is called for."

"Meaning?"

"Persistence and patience," he recommended. "Whatever you've done to rattle him, do that and more of it." An unrepentant grin suddenly crossed his face. "Ah, here is the very man in question, looking oddly unrefreshed from his nap."

"Go to hell," Ryan muttered as he crossed to the

coffeepot and poured himself a cup. Only then did he glance at Maggie. "Want some?"

"I'd love a cup," she said, noting that Ryan's gaze fell on Rosita as he poured the coffee. He hesitated, then gave a resigned shake of his head before handing Maggie her coffee.

"Okay," Rory declared, "there are too many people in my kitchen. You two, out. I'll fix you an omelette and bring it out, or would you prefer a sandwich since we're well into afternoon now?"

"An omelette sounds lovely," Maggie said.

"Perhaps Rosita could fix it," Ryan suggested.

"She's on a break," Rory retorted emphatically.

"Come on," Maggie encouraged before Ryan could debate the topic.

"I knew hiring that woman was a mistake the instant I saw she was pregnant," he complained as they went to a booth. "If nothing else, Rory is gallant. I knew he'd never let her do a lick of work."

"If it's any consolation, I think Rosita is as frustrated as you are."

"That doesn't actually help. I hired her because Rory claimed to need help."

"And now he's satisfied. Maybe all he really needed was company."

"I am not paying someone to sit in there and chat with him. Besides, she doesn't know enough English to carry on a conversation."

"Oh, I think she knows enough," Maggie said, then captured and held his gaze. "So, Rory tells me you slept down here. Mind telling me why?"

"I sat down for a minute and fell asleep," he said defensively. "There's nothing more to it."

"But why were you down here in the first place? You were as exhausted as I was. I thought you were going straight to sleep on the sofa upstairs."

He shrugged. "I changed my mind."

"I hope it wasn't because of me."

He didn't look away as she'd anticipated. Instead, he turned the challenge around.

"Now why would you have anything to do with it?" he asked.

"Oh, I don't know," she said with an offhand shrug. "Maybe because you were tempted to crawl into your bed with me."

"Absolutely not," he said.

Maggie laughed at the too-quick response. "Liar, but I'm going to let that pass this time."

"How gracious of you," he said sourly. "Did you explain to your mother that I couldn't come to dinner?"

"She wasn't home. I left her a message to that effect. Just to prepare you, though, don't be surprised if she comes in here to demand an explanation."

He frowned at that. "Can't anyone in your family take a simple no for an answer?"

"Not usually," she said cheerfully. "You should probably try to get used to it."

"Why? Eventually you'll go back to Maine, and that will be that. I'll probably never see you or any of your family again."

Maggie shook her head at the note of resignation in his voice. "That's not how it works with us. Face it, Devaney, we're here to stay."

"What about Maine?" he asked, a faint note of desperation in his voice. Apparently, he'd been clinging to the notion that she would be leaving after the holidays so he could let himself off the hook and never have to deal with his all-too-apparent feelings for her.

"I've decided not to go back," she announced, making the decision on the spot. Whatever happened between her and Ryan, she wanted to remain in Boston. And, if she had her way, she would work right here, by his side. Eventually maybe he'd even let her get her hands on his accounting system so she could bring him into the twenty-first century.

His gaze narrowed. "Why not?"

"There's nothing for me there," she said.

"And here?"

"That remains to be seen."

Ryan sighed heavily at her response, but Maggie was almost certain there was a slight flicker of relief in his eyes. It wasn't much, but she was going to cling to that with everything she had.

• • •

A week later, with Christmas only days away, Ryan was still cursing the fact that he hadn't done everything he could to persuade Maggie that she belonged in Maine. The only trouble would have been that he didn't believe it. It was more and more evident to him that she belonged right here, making him laugh with her stories about her family.

Making him yearn.

Even so, he caught himself before he allowed her to weave a spell around him that couldn't be broken. Though the invitations to join the O'Briens for dinner came almost daily, he determinedly turned down every single one. He was pretty sure he was finally getting through to Maggie that what they had now was as far as he was going to allow things to go.

Of course, just when he was feeling confident, he looked up and spotted her mother coming through the pub's door with a determined glint in her eyes. Maggie had warned him about precisely this, but as the days had gone by, he'd put the possibility of a direct confrontation with Nell O'Brien from his mind. Now, on Christmas Eve, she was standing squarely in front of him, hands on hips and a no-nonsense expression on her face.

"I am going to pretend that you haven't rudely turned down every single invitation Maggie's offered," she said, eyes flashing. "I will not allow you to say no to having Christmas dinner with us tomorrow. Father Francis is invited, as well."

"The shelter—" Ryan began, only to have his words cut off.

"Dinner at the shelter is at noon. I checked," she told him. "We'll eat at five. That should give you both plenty of time to get there." She tilted her head in a way that reminded him of Maggie. "Any questions?"

Ryan knew when he was beaten. "No, ma'am."

"Then I'll see you tomorrow?"

"Yes, thank you. Can I bring anything?"

"Just Father Francis and a pleasant attitude," she said, then kissed his cheek. "And a small token for Maggie, perhaps. I know she has a little something for you."

Ryan sighed. He'd already seen the perfect gift for Maggie, but he'd kept himself from buying it. He'd told himself that any present at all would carry implications of a connection he was trying not to encourage. He should have known it was another bad decision on his part, should have realized that she would have no such reticence about buying him something.

"Maureen, watch the bar," he called to his waitress. "I have an errand to run."

"We're filled to overflowing and you want to run an errand?" she asked, regarding him with astonishment.

"Last-minute Christmas shopping," he said.

A grin spread across her face. "And if I'm not mistaken, that was Maggie O'Brien's mother who just came breezing through here. Does that mean you're going to buy something special for Maggie?"

"You can jump to whatever conclusions you want," he said, "as long as I can get out of here before the stores close."

"Go," Maureen said. "Besides, I imagine Maggie will be along any minute now to help out. Shall I tell her you're out shopping for her?"

He scowled. "You'll do no such thing, or your bonus for this year will turn out to be ashes and switches."

Maureen laughed at the empty threat. "You gave me my bonus last week."

He sighed. "Next year, then."

As if the holidays weren't stressful enough for him, why was it that every female he knew had suddenly decided this was the perfect season to drive him crazy?

Chapter Eleven

"It's a good thing you're doing," Father Francis assured Ryan as they drove to Maggie's house on Christmas afternoon after a busy morning at the shelter during which Ryan had played Santa to dozens of children. "It's about time you spent a holiday with a real family, rather than just the lost souls at the shelter or the strays who wander into the pub."

"This from a man who is usually among those strays," Ryan retorted.

"Only because I worry about you," the priest responded. "And because Rory is the only man I know who can make a decent Christmas pudding."

"Then why are you so agreeable to missing it this year?" Ryan asked.

"Because we've had a better offer. Christmas pudding is not the most important part of the holiday, after all."

"Besides which, I'm sure Rory agreed to save you some," Ryan guessed.

"Aye, that he did," the priest agreed unrepentantly.

A few minutes later Ryan found a parking space half a block from the O'Brien home. Judging from the number of cars in front of the house and lining the driveway, there was a full house. Even though he was likely to know almost everyone there, Ryan suffered a moment of panic at the prospect of facing them. However, one look from Father Francis had him cutting the engine and climbing out.

At the door Maggie greeted them warmly, reserving a smug grin for Ryan. "They've been taking bets inside on whether you'd show up," she told him. "I believe my haul should be more than twenty dollars. Mother gets the other half."

"Do you all bet on everything?" he asked as Father Francis laughed.

"Just about," she said, standing on tiptoe to give Ryan a slow, deliberate kiss that made his head spin.

Before he could gather his wits, Ryan heard Father Francis mutter, "About time." Then the priest disappeared in an obvious attempt to give them some privacy.

Ryan felt Maggie's lips curve into a slow smile against his. When he pulled away, there was amusement dancing in her eyes. "What?" he demanded crankily.

"Nothing," she insisted. "Did you hear me say a word?"

Ryan gave a nod of satisfaction. "Keep it that way. This situation is not amusing, Maggie. I can't seem to make myself stay away from you, but that doesn't mean I've changed my mind. I'm the wrong man for you."

She surveyed him so thoroughly he almost squirmed, then shook her head. “I don’t see it.”

“See what?”

“You being wrong for me.” Her gaze lit on the small gift bag in his hand. “Is that for me?”

With a sigh, he handed it to her. A part of him wanted her to open the present right then, but a part of him dreaded it. He didn’t have a lot of practice picking out gifts, but this one had seemed so right. If she hated it, he was going to feel like an idiot.

Maggie had no such hesitations. She was pulling tissue from the bag with the excitement of a child. Her eyes lit up when she saw the small, square box. For a moment she fumbled with the lid, then impatiently handed it to him. “I’m all thumbs. You open it.”

“It’s your present,” he protested.

“Please.”

Ryan took the box, slit the tape holding it closed, then lifted the lid just enough to make opening it the rest of the way easy for her. “Okay, all yours,” he said, anxious to be rid of it. Even so, he couldn’t tear his gaze away as he awaited her reaction.

Maggie carefully unfolded the tissue in the box, then sighed. “Oh, my,” she whispered, her eyes shining. “Ryan, they’re beautiful.” She removed the antique marcasite hair clips from the box with a look of reverence. The clips were made in the shape of shamrocks, and each had a tiny emerald chip in the center that was the exact color of Maggie's eyes. "I have to put them on."

Ryan stood as if frozen while she moved to a mirror on the foyer wall. Once the sparkling clips were in her hair, she turned to him with a smile. "They're perfect, the very best present anyone ever gave me. Thank you."

Ryan didn't know how to cope with either her gratitude or the too-obvious love shining in her eyes. It was all too much for a man who'd rarely been the recipient of either, at least not from anyone who'd truly mattered. Panic rushed through him. Not five minutes ago he'd told her that he was wrong for her, and now, apparently, she was more convinced than ever that they were exactly right for each other. He'd never realized before that a gift could speak volumes, could even contradict words, no matter how emphatically they'd been expressed.

"Maggie, I'm sorry. I can't do this," he said, turning toward the door. Before he could bolt, however, she stepped in front of him.

"Do what?" she asked.

He gestured toward the rest of the house, which was crowded with O'Briens. "The family thing. I'm no good at it."

Her gaze locked with his, unrelenting, yet tempered with understanding. "If that's true—and I'm not saying I believe it for a minute—then it's time you told me why. The whole story, not bits and snatches."

Ryan sighed at her reasonable request. "Yes, I do owe you an explanation, but not today. Your family's waiting for you in there."

"They're waiting for both of us," she corrected. "There are plenty of appetizers and Dad's eggnog. They won't mind waiting a little longer."

So, he thought, this was it. "Is there someplace we can talk privately?"

"My room," she said at once.

Ryan balked as if she'd suggested going upstairs to make love. "I am not going to your room with you, in front of your entire family. Are you nuts? What will they think?"

"That we're looking for someplace private," she replied reasonably. "In case you haven't noticed, there's a crowd in the kitchen keeping my mom company while she cooks. There's a crowd in the den watching football. The kids are in the rec room downstairs. And there are at least a half dozen people in the living room listening to every word we're saying right now. Do you have a better idea?"

He latched on to her hand, grabbed a coat off the rack by the door and dragged her outside to his car. He turned the heater up full blast, then turned to look at her. Only then did he realize that he'd mistakenly grabbed a coat belonging to someone much larger. She looked lost and more delicate than ever in the folds of dark-blue wool. Her wide eyes watched him warily as if she were uncertain what sort of storm she'd unleashed.

Before he could drag her to him and kiss her the way he desperately wanted to, he forced himself to take a deep breath and tell her everything—about the way his parents had run off, about the devastating day he'd been separated from his brothers, about the roller-coaster ride he'd taken through the foster care system, about Father Francis catching him just as he'd been about to break into a neighborhood quick-mart for something to eat on a bitterly cold Thanksgiving eve.

"It wasn't the first time I'd broken into a store, and probably wouldn't have been the last," he told her, his gaze unflinching. "I was a thief."

"You were a hungry kid," she countered, her eyes overflowing with sympathetic tears.

"Don't excuse what I did because you feel sorry for me," he retorted sharply, hating that she seemed so eager to overlook the truth. "And don't you dare pity me. I didn't deserve it then, and I certainly don't now. I knew right from wrong."

"You were a boy," she insisted, still fiercely defending him. "You were obviously desperate."

"I was old enough to know better," he countered just as harshly. "I was just a no-good brat. Obviously, my parents knew that." He took a deep breath, then blurted the secret guilt he'd kept hidden in his heart for so long. "It's why they left, why I could never fit in with any of the foster families."

Maggie stared at him in shocked disbelief. "No," she said, flatly refusing to accept his explanation. "Whatever the reason your parents left, it wasn't that."

Ryan was startled by the depth of her conviction. He wished he were half as convinced that he'd had no role to play in their leaving. What else was he to think, though? He'd been the oldest. If only he'd taken on more responsibility, behaved better, perhaps things would have been different.

"I've asked this before, but you've avoided answering. Have you ever tried to find them or your brothers?" she asked, her voice suddenly gentle.

He shook his head.

"I've asked before, but I'll ask it again—why not?"

"Isn't it obvious? They wanted no part of me or my brothers. Why should I go crawling after them?"

"If it were me, I'd want to know why they did it," she said simply. "I'd have to know."

"Some things defy explanation."

"And some things are less painful when you're old enough to understand the truth."

"That's nothing more than a bunch of psychological mumbo-jumbo and you know it," he accused. "I don't need it."

"Then what *do* you need from me?"

He regarded her sadly. "Nothing," he insisted, lying through his teeth. "Absolutely nothing."

Maggie didn't say a word, but she looked shattered. Before he realized what she intended, she was out of the car and running up the sidewalk. Ryan sat there, the open passenger door letting in the freezing air, and realized that never, not even on the day he'd been abandoned by his parents, had he felt quite so alone.

The pounding on the door to his apartment would have awakened the dead. Ryan scowled but didn't budge from his chair. The drink he'd poured himself when he'd returned from Maggie's was still full. Even as he'd filled the glass, he'd known the solution to his problems wasn't alcohol. Unless he drank the whole blasted bottle it wouldn't grant him the oblivion he sought.

"Dammit, I know you're in there," Rory shouted. "Open the door or I'll have to break it down."

Ryan sighed. He knew Rory was not only capable of such a thing but, given the heat in his voice, probably even eager to do it. He crossed the room in three long strides and threw open the door.

"What is your problem?" he demanded.

"I'm not the one with the problem," Rory said.

"Oh?"

"Maggie called. She's worried about you."

"She shouldn't be," Ryan said.

"Then call her and tell her that."

"I don't think so." As horrendous as this pain in his chest was, he knew that dragging Maggie back into his life wasn't going to work. It was better that they end this with a clean break.

Rory noted the glass of scotch beside his chair. "I thought you didn't drink."

"I *rarely* drink. There's a difference," Ryan said. "And if you nose around a little more closely, you'll see that I haven't touched that drink, either."

Rory gave a nod. "That's okay, then. Want to talk about what happened?"

"No."

"Interesting. Maggie didn't say much, either."

"How discreet of her," Ryan said sarcastically. "It's a pleasant change."

Rory frowned at him then. "Maligning Maggie won't fix whatever's bugging you."

"Don't you think I know that?"

"Talking it out might help."

"I am *not* discussing this, not with you, not with Maggie," Ryan said forcefully, his gaze leveled at his friend. "Are we clear on that?"

"Whatever you say," Rory said. "I suppose I'm expected to call her and tell her you're still among the living?"

Ryan shrugged. "Up to you."

"Perhaps I should drive out to console her," Rory suggested slyly.

Ryan felt his gut tighten. "Don't expect me to object."

"Okay, that's it," Rory declared, plopping down on the sofa. "I'm not leaving here until you tell me what happened. The day you say it's okay for me to pay a visit to Maggie is obviously the next-to-last day of the world."

Despite his foul mood, Ryan felt his lips twitch. "It's nothing that dire. It's just that it's over," he told Rory, keeping his tone surprisingly even. "Not that there was anything to begin with, just the promise of something."

"And you ended it, I suppose."

Ryan thought back over the scene outside of Maggie's. He'd said the words that had ended it, but it was Maggie who'd walked away. There was equal blame, if he wanted to be honest about it. No, he corrected, the blame was all his. He'd done what he was so good at doing. He'd shut her out, this time with a declaration she couldn't ignore.

"Yeah, I suppose I ended it," he admitted.

"Why the devil would you do a lame-brained thing like that?" Rory demanded, clearly dumbstruck. "And on Christmas, too? Have you no heart at all?"

Ryan met his friend's scowling gaze. "No," he said evenly. "And isn't that the point?"

"Sure, and if that's so, then why does it appear to me that it's not your hard head that's suffering so tonight? It seems to me it's your heart that's broken," Rory said, then headed for the door. "Think about that one, why don't you?"

When the door clicked shut, Ryan closed his eyes against the tide of anguish and regret washing over him. He tried once again telling himself that he'd done the right thing, but being in the right was cold comfort.

The remainder of Christmas day passed in a blur for Maggie. She managed to keep a smile on her face, but she didn't really fool anyone. She knew, because they all tiptoed around Ryan's sudden disappearance, not a one of them asking why he'd gone. Matt quietly offered Father Francis a lift back to the city, and the priest left after giving Maggie's hand a sympathetic squeeze. Obviously, not even he intended to try to explain away Ryan's abrupt departure. Of course, Maggie already knew the answer to that. He'd left because he couldn't bear to spend another minute in her company . . . and because she'd run at the first sign of trouble.

The fact that her call to Rory had been as pointless as every other attempt to get through to Ryan only made her heartache worse. He'd called back to confirm that Ryan had gotten home, adding nothing more, not even a glimmer of hope that

Ryan's brooding state was likely to change come morning.

After several restless, sleepless nights, by the following Monday morning Maggie had convinced herself that *she* ought to search for the Devaneys if Ryan wasn't going to do it. They were the key to this.

Downstairs, though, in the clear light of day, she knew that finding Ryan's family wasn't up to her. No matter how important she thought it was for Ryan to confront the past, he was the only one who could make the decision to do so.

"Maggie?" her mother said, studying her worriedly. "What's troubling you? I haven't wanted to pry, but did you and Ryan have a fight the other day? Is that why he left?"

Had it been a fight? Not really. He'd simply told her he didn't need her, that he never would. She'd walked away without a word.

"No," she said wearily, stirring sugar into the tea her mother set in front of her.

"Then what?"

"I can't talk about it, not just yet," she said.

"I saw the hair clips he gave you. They're lovely."

Maggie smiled. "Aren't they? He couldn't have picked a more perfect gift."

"Did you give him his present?"

She shook her head. "I never had the chance."

"Will you take it to him?"

"I honestly don't know."

"Because you don't want to be the one to take the first step toward mending fences? Pride's a lonely bedfellow," her mother reminded her. "If it were me, I'd take it today and resolve whatever disagreement you had so you can start the new year fresh."

Maggie sighed. It wasn't pride that had her considering staying away from the pub. It was a matter of protecting her aching heart.

But deep inside, she knew that staying away was impossible. The two most important people in Ryan's life had turned their backs on him at a critical time. She was not about to be just another person who loved him and let him down.

And she did love him. She'd accepted that weeks ago. She'd also accepted that she'd found her niche at the pub. She liked working side by side with Ryan. She loved making the customers feel welcome, loved the homey feel of the place, the impromptu singing that livened the atmosphere on many a night. Who would have thought that Father Francis would have a voice like an angel?

Maggie was not going to give up any of that without a fight. She stood up, then bent to kiss her mother's cheek. "Thanks."

"For what?"

"For reminding me what's important," she said.

"Did I do that?" her mother inquired innocently.

Maggie grinned. “You and Dad do that every day, just by being who you are.”

A serene smile stole across her mother’s face. “If we’ve given you an understanding of what marriage can be at its full potential, then we’ve done well by you. Now run along. I have faith that you can teach Ryan the same lesson with a little patience and a lot of love.”

“I hope so,” Maggie said. “Because I do love him, Mom.”

Her mother gave her a hug. “I know you do. I also know he probably doesn’t make it easy. But if you ask me, he returns those feelings. I just don’t think he recognizes it quite yet, perhaps because it’s such a new experience for him.”

Maggie thought about her mother’s words on the drive into Boston. She held tightly to them as she braced herself, put on a sunny smile and walked into the pub as if she’d never been away. She dropped his present casually on the bar, then moved on to hang up her coat. Before she turned away she saw the surprise in Ryan’s eyes and something else, possibly a hint of relief.

Determined to act as if nothing were amiss, she grabbed her apron and immediately went to work, grateful that the place was packed and she could delay actually speaking to Ryan.

When Maureen caught up with her, she said, “Maggie, thank God you’re back.”

“I can see you’re swamped,” Maggie said.

"It's not the crowds I can't handle, it's Ryan. He's been grouchy as a bear since Christmas. It's a wonder he hasn't driven all the customers away, to say nothing of the staff. Even Rory's giving him a wide berth."

That news gave Maggie more confidence. When she eventually passed behind the bar, Ryan caught her hand and held her still, his blue eyes searching her face.

"I'm sorry for what happened on Christmas," he said finally. "I behaved like an idiot."

She studied his dear, familiar face and saw the genuine remorse. She touched a hand to his cheek. "I know."

"I'm glad you came back."

She permitted herself a small smile. "I know that, too."

He drew in a deep breath as if gathering his courage, then declared, "I've had nothing to do but think the past few days, and I've come to a conclusion. I want you, Maggie O'Brien, and if you say you know that, as well, I'll have to kiss you, right here in front of everyone."

Her smile spread. "I know everything about you, Ryan Devaney. Get used to it."

It was tantamount to a dare and they both knew it. Heat flared in his eyes right before his mouth covered hers. This was no coaxing, tentative kiss. It was a crushing, demanding kiss that had her blood turning to fire. The new urgency and neediness turned the kiss even more dangerous than all the others that had gone before. His tongue swept inside her mouth, and Maggie felt the world spin.

The only thing that stopped the kiss from lasting an eternity was the cheer that erupted from the entire bar. Ryan backed away from her as if he'd been burned.

"I'm sorry," he said, his voice husky.

Maggie scowled at his words. "Don't you dare apologize," she said.

He grinned at the ferocity of her response. "We'll finish this later," he promised.

"The kiss or the discussion?"

"Probably both," he admitted with a rueful grin.

It was all the opening she needed. Maggie's gaze locked with his. "It could be a good night to close early," she suggested with a wink.

Ryan shook his head, suddenly all practicality and reason, as he grabbed a cloth and began polishing the bar. "Monday-night football."

She'd already learned not to let reason kick in with him. It kept him safe, not alive the way a man should be. He needed to work on his spontaneity.

She glanced around at the sea of mostly familiar faces and said loudly, "Don't any of these people have televisions at home?"

The question was greeted with laughter and a sudden flurry of activity, and the place cleared out in ten minutes flat. Even Maureen had vanished with a promise to come in early to count the receipts in the morning.

"You can sleep in," she said to Ryan with a wink.

After Maureen had gone, locking the door behind her, Ryan gazed around with a stunned expression, then faced Maggie with feigned indignation. "You trying to ruin my business?"

She shook her head. "Nope. Just trying to get your clothes off."

He swallowed hard at that, then turned out all the lights except for the neon shamrock in the window, picked up his unopened gift and grabbed her hand. "Well, then, since it looks as if I have the night off, let's go upstairs and see what we can do about that."

Maggie gave him a considering look. "What's wrong with right here?"

"You want me to strip in the middle of the pub?"

"I'm a risk taker. How about you?"

"The condoms are upstairs."

Maggie hesitated, then glanced around the room with regret. "I'm not that much of a risk taker. Upstairs it is."

"Don't look so sad," Ryan teased. "I'll make it worth your while."

She grinned at him. "I'm counting on it."

Chapter Twelve

Ryan kept expecting to wake up from a dream. Instead, each brush of Maggie's hands over his chest, each deeply satisfying kiss, felt very real. The roar of his blood, the heat generated by each caress, the demanding need, couldn't possibly have been matched by a mere dream, no matter how sweet.

He opened his eyes, saw the flesh-and-blood Maggie before him and knew the greatest sense of satisfaction he'd ever felt in his life. This—*she*—was real. She was in his arms, just as she was in his heart.

For better or for worse.

Right now, though, he could only think of the positives, of the way the light turned her pale skin a soft gold, the way her curves fit him, the way she came alive with each touch, the way her back arched when he cupped her breast in the palm of his hand.

There was nothing halfway about Maggie. She was open and giving, and demanded as much as she gave.

Ryan lifted his head and gazed into her sea-green eyes. "You are a revelation."

"Oh?" She eyed him with sleepy sensuality. "What were you expecting?"

"Caution. Restraint. A hint of modesty, perhaps."

She laughed. "From me? I've been all but begging for this moment for weeks now. There wasn't much caution or restraint in that."

He gave her a sheepish shrug. "I honestly thought it was all talk."

"Are you disappointed that it wasn't?" she asked, a faint hint of worry in her eyes.

Ryan pressed a kiss at the base of her throat, felt the quick flash of heat beneath his lips. "Absolutely not. An eager woman can be a real turn-on, especially when it's unexpected."

She grinned at that. "Then you won't mind if I do this," she said, reaching for the snap on his jeans. "I think this break has lasted long enough."

Ryan jerked as her knuckles skimmed his abdomen. With her gaze locked with his, she lowered the zipper on his jeans, then slid them down his legs. He kicked them aside.

"Anything else you're anxious to strip off me?" he inquired in a lazy tone, curious to see what she'd do next.

"Those shorts have to go sooner or later," she said with a considering look that sent his temperature soaring. She lifted her gaze to his, a half smile on her lips. "But not just yet."

Ryan couldn't breathe. "Oh?"

"Don't think I don't know the fine art of building anticipation, Ryan Devaney. Haven't I been patient for weeks now, while you've been making up your mind? Hasn't it almost driven me to distraction?"

"Really?" he asked, pleased beyond measure that she'd been as anxious as he for this moment. "You've had your revenge, though. You've done your best to torment me every minute."

"Well, of course I have," she said smugly. "Isn't that the point? How else was I to make you want me so desperately you'd forget all your silly reservations?"

His mood sobered at once at the teasing question. "They weren't silly, Maggie. And I still have a slew of them."

She shook her head. "Not tonight, you don't. And tonight is all that matters. One night, Ryan." She grinned. "And then possibly another."

It was the give-an-inch-take-a-mile attitude with which he'd become increasingly familiar, and which had made him increasingly wary.

"I can't promise tomorrow," he said, needing to be clear about that even though he'd begun dreaming of weeks and months from now.

"Have I asked you to?" she inquired lightly.

"No," he admitted. "But you deserve all the promises of tomorrow a man can make."

"If it's right, they'll come in time," she said readily. "For now, I think it's best if we concentrate on the moment."

She lifted her sweater over her head, then shimmied out of her jeans, revealing all the fancy, delicate lace he'd fantasized about. She might tend toward an unremarkable wardrobe of sedate jeans and sweaters, but beneath she clearly indulged her feminine side.

Her body was perfect with its narrow hips, long, long legs and breasts that filled the cups of her bra to overflowing. He could have stared at her forever, but she was having none of that. She moved closer, looped her arms around his neck and hooked one leg around his, bringing all that satiny skin and heat in contact with his own suddenly burning flesh.

"Make love to me, Ryan," she whispered against his lips. "Now."

He pushed aside the last nagging cautions, lifted her up and settled her on his bed. Then he stripped off his shorts and joined her, making quick work of getting rid of those remaining scraps of lace. For the moment he was content to explore every inch of her with lingering caresses, discovering the secrets of her body, his gaze locked on her expressive face as her arousal grew and her movements turned restless.

"Now," she pleaded, her back arching, her hips lifting off the bed in time to the rhythm of his fingers probing deep inside her. "Please, Ryan. I want you inside me."

"It's okay," he said as her body tensed. "Go with it, darlin'. Let it come."

"But—" The rest of the protest was lost as the climax ripped through her.

Only when the last shudder had died away did he slowly enter her, thrusting deep, then waiting as her body adjusted to him. The welcoming heat wrapped itself around him, and her last fluttering contractions made him even harder.

Then, looking into her eyes, he began to move, the steady, pulsing rhythm as old as time as it built to a higher and higher peak. The wonder on Maggie's face would have been enough, but there was more. There were the sweet cries deep in her throat, the demanding rise of her hips to meet his, the glow of perspiration on her skin as she strained to reach that elusive, final pinnacle. Her eyes drifted closed, as if to increase her concentration on the struggle, but Ryan was having none of that, not when they were so close to the end.

"Maggie, look at me," he commanded. He needed to know that she was with *him* and no one else. He could feel her body starting to shudder, could feel his own tensing for one last thrust and an exquisite release. "Look at me!"

She opened her eyes just as the rush of his climax rocked through him. Her hips rose one last time, and then she, too, was catapulting over the brink.

The aftershocks seemed to go on forever. Ryan rolled on his back and pulled her on top of him, cradling her close, as his breathing finally slowed. Maggie was limp in his arms, her own breathing ragged.

Eventually she lifted her head and met his gaze. "That was . . . remarkable."

Ryan grinned at the stunned note in her voice. "I told you I'd make coming upstairs worth your while."

Her mouth gaped at the reminder, and then, to his shock, she began to laugh.

"What?" he asked, bemused by the reaction. He'd certainly found nothing to laugh about in the last hour or more.

"We came up for the condoms," she reminded him.

A sense of dismay washed over him at the implication. "And forgot them," he said slowly. "Oh, my God, Maggie, I'm sorry. It never crossed my mind."

"Nor mine," she reminded him.

"But I'm always responsible." He raked a hand through his hair. What had he been thinking? Of course, that was precisely the problem, he hadn't been thinking. Not with his brain, anyway. And the rest of his anatomy clearly wasn't to be trusted. What the hell was he supposed to do if she got pregnant? He couldn't—he wouldn't—abandon her. But what kind of father could he possibly be? What kind of husband? All of the questions he'd spend a lifetime thinking he'd never have to deal with came crashing down around him, demanding answers.

Even as the questions set off panic, a tiny part of him marveled at the possibility that they had created a child together. The fear of committing to that—to Maggie—wasn't nearly as horrendous as it would have been even days ago.

Maggie touched a finger to his brow. "Uh-oh. Worry lines. Stop it, Ryan. I'm not going to get pregnant."

"You can't possibly know that. People get pregnant all the time, even when they use protection."

"Well, it won't be your problem if I do," she insisted, her jaw set stubbornly.

If that was meant to be reassuring, it failed miserably. Instead, it infuriated him. "And whose would it be? Is there someone in this bed I'm not aware of?"

"I just meant—"

"I know what you meant. You're trying to let me off the hook . . . again," he said, all but shouting. "And let's get one thing very clear, if there's a baby, I'm responsible. It *is* my problem, and we'll deal with it together. Understood?"

"I won't have you trapped into a marriage you don't want, Ryan," she said, her voice cool. "That's something you need to understand. Any baby we conceived wouldn't be a problem, not to me. It would be a blessing." She regarded him wistfully. "Do we have to fight about this now?"

"Isn't it better to be clear about things now, rather than put them off till we've a crisis?" he asked.

"No," she said emphatically. "Because I've just had the best night of my life, and you're ruining it with all this talk of doom and gloom." She frowned at him. "Now let me be clear about something—I won't have it."

He grinned despite himself. "Okay then, no more doom and gloom. Would I be out of line if I suggested another kiss?"

"Perhaps." Her expression turned thoughtful. "Try it and we'll see."

"I prefer not to take chances, especially with a woman who's in such a dangerous mood."

She laughed, and the dark mood was broken for good. "Come here and kiss me."

He chuckled and rolled toward the nightstand. "If you don't mind, I think I'll grab the condoms first. With you, one kiss has a way of leading to another."

Maggie had waited so long for this moment she thought her heart would burst from sheer joy. She was not going to allow Ryan's momentary panic about the possibility of a baby ruin it. Truthfully, she could think of nothing more wonderful than having his child, but she could understand his fears.

To her those fears were just one more reason

why he needed to act and do whatever it took to put the past to rest, but she was done with nudging him. It hadn't gotten her anywhere so far.

She rolled over and stared at him, admiring his long, lean body and well-defined muscles.

"Is there something here you like?" he inquired, his voice threaded with amusement.

"I'm debating," she said.

"Very funny."

She met his gaze then, her expression serious. "Did I mention to you that last night was the best night of my life?"

"Once or twice," he teased.

"Well, it was, and I see no point in denying it."

He grinned. "I'd be the last one to want you to. So, Miss Maggie, what plans do you have for the day? The new year is fast approaching. Have you given any thought to what you'll be doing come January?"

"Trying to get rid of me?" she asked, attempting to inject a light note into her voice. But even she could hear the hint of edginess.

"Never that," he said, his expression unguarded for once. "I want you here, Maggie. More than I should."

She relaxed then, relieved that he'd asked, after a fashion, anyway. "Then this is where I'll be."

He studied her. "For how long?"

"Now who's pushing for more than one day at a

time?" she teased. "Is it a commitment you're asking for, Ryan Devaney?"

He seemed to struggle with himself before finally sighing. "What if I were?"

"Then you'd have it," she said without any hesitation at all.

He seemed taken aback by her ready response. "Just like that?"

"Just like that." She regarded him with a steady look. "But you're not asking yet, are you?"

He reached over and brushed a wayward curl from her cheek. "Not yet, Maggie," he said with obvious regret. "But I'm beginning to believe that one of these days I will."

She rose on one elbow to kiss him. "Then I'll be waiting for that day. And in the meantime, I'll be poking into your business at the pub as much as you'll let me."

He chuckled. "Which won't be much," he warned.

"We'll see."

"Aren't the books at St. Mary's enough to keep you occupied?"

"Hardly. I had those straightened up the first week. The only thing giving me any trouble is getting Father Francis to follow the rules about collecting receipts for what he buys for the shelter and taking note of the donations so a proper acknowledgment can be sent."

"I can see where that might be a challenge," he

said. "Since he's not a stupid man, has it occurred to you that he's being impossible just to make sure you keep coming around?"

Truthfully that had never crossed Maggie's mind. "You think so?"

"If it were me, I would."

She grinned at him. "In other words, you won't let me touch your business records because you're holding them in reserve as an incentive to keep me here?"

"You never know," he teased.

"What if I were to promise to stick around, anyway—would you let me work on them then?"

He seemed to consider the question thoughtfully, then shook his head. "Afraid not."

"Why not?"

He shrugged. "Too much experience with broken promises."

Maggie sighed. They were back to his family again. "Ryan—"

He held up a hand. "No. Don't go there. For once, let's just forget all about my family."

"Okay," she said with a nod of agreement. "I can do that." She leveled a look directly into his eyes. "Can you?"

Maggie's challenge lingered in Ryan's head for days. He knew he was in way over his head with Maggie if he was even considering for a second looking for his parents. And he *was* thinking about it, not because he wanted to find them, but because it mattered so damned much to her. He'd give her just about anything on earth she wanted. From the moment he'd made love to her, he'd known he was lost.

With her open, generous heart, Maggie offered everything he'd been denied all his life—love, a sense of belonging, joy. And with Nell and Garrett O'Brien and the others, she was also offering him the chance to be connected to a real family. That should have been more than enough for a man who'd had so little in the way of love.

But as happy as he was with their growing relationship, he was forced to admit that there was still something missing from his life, something that Maggie could never replace. Perhaps, if he was brave enough, they could marry and have children, but no matter how many people she brought into his life, it would never entirely make up for those he'd lost. From the moment she'd uttered that challenge, she hadn't said anything more about finding his family, but she, too, clearly believed that they were the missing part of his heart. If he hadn't known it before, he couldn't mistake it once he'd finally opened her Christmas present—a frame with his picture and room for five more. He'd known those empty spaces were meant for photos of his brothers and parents.

Despite all that, Ryan couldn't seem to bring

himself to do anything about initiating a search. He wasn't entirely sure why he was so terrified to try. Was he afraid of being disappointed? Or afraid of another rejection?

Whenever his head was filled with questions and no answers, he always headed for the shelter. There were people there with worse problems than his, people who survived despite whatever tragedies had befallen them.

When he arrived at midmorning, he was surprised to find Letitia at work in the kitchen preparing lunch for the children. She was making peanut butter and jelly sandwiches at a rapid clip, but her expression was distracted.

"Everything okay?" Ryan inquired after watching her for several minutes.

She looked up from her task, and her face broke into a smile. "Mr. Devaney, what are you doing here?"

"I came by to spend some time with the kids. They usually need a distraction during the holidays. With no school and some of the parents out looking for jobs, they can get a little rambunctious. What are you doing here? I thought you'd be at the hospital."

"Jamal's with Lamar." Her eyes lit up. "Did you know he's getting out of the hospital later this week? The doctors say he's making fantastic progress. Looks like my boy has a bright future ahead of him."

"That's wonderful. Will you be coming back here?"

She shook her head, her smile widening. "Jamal went back to his old boss and explained what had happened. He agreed to take him back after the first of the year. He even gave him an advance on his salary, so we could make a deposit on an apartment. We move in tomorrow so we can get it all fixed up before Lamar comes home."

She put down the jar of jelly and crossed the room to hug him. "I have my life back, and it's all because of you."

Ryan was growing more comfortable with the impulsive show of affection, but not with the praise. "Letitia—" he began.

She cut off his protest. "I won't hear none of that," she scolded. "You did a good thing. Now accept my thanks."

He grinned. "You're welcome."

She studied him intently. "Is there something else on your mind? You've got the look of a man with troubles. Is it Maggie?"

"Maggie's fine," he said.

"You treating her right?"

He grinned at the protective note in her voice. "As right as I know how."

"What's that mean?"

"It's a long story. I won't bore you with it."

She frowned at that. "Let me get these sandwiches out to my babies out there, and you tell me the story."

Oddly, Ryan couldn't seem to make himself turn down the offer. Maybe what he needed was an entirely fresh perspective. For so long now he'd simply tuned out Father Francis's advice and, more recently, even Maggie's, because he hadn't wanted to deal with the past at all.

Letitia made short work of delivering lunch to the children in the dining room, then came back and poured them each a cup of coffee. "Now sit down over here and tell me what's on your mind," she instructed him in a no-nonsense tone.

Ryan began the story with the day his parents left and he was separated from his brothers. Tears welled up in Letitia's eyes as he talked, but she didn't say a word. She just listened until he had told her everything, right on up to Maggie's belief that he needed to find his family if he was ever to have any real peace.

"I'm beginning to think she's right," he admitted. "I've been living in some sort of emotional limbo for too long now."

"Seems that way to me, too," Letitia said. "And there's one more thing you're not considering."

"What's that?"

"Just think for a minute about what happened to Lamar because his daddy and I didn't know Jamal's medical history and what it could mean for our boy. You haven't said if you're thinking of marrying Maggie, but if that thought has crossed your mind, you need to know something about this whole genetics thing."

Ryan seized on that as if he'd been presented with a lifeline. "You're absolutely right," he told Letitia. For the first time, he had a purely practical reason for conducting a search for his family—one he could embrace without risking his heart.

Letitia looked troubled by his reaction. "That shouldn't be the only reason you go looking for them," she cautioned, as if she'd read his mind.

"I know," he acknowledged, but it was reason enough. A nice, *safe* reason. He stood up and bent down to kiss her cheek. "Thank you."

"I didn't do a thing," she said.

Ryan grinned at her. "Accept my thanks graciously," he chided.

Letitia laughed. "It's good to see a man who's not too old to learn a thing or two. Now, get on out of here and take care of business. And remember—I expect an invitation to the wedding."

He hesitated at the suggestion. "I never said anything about a wedding."

"The day will come," she said confidently. "Unless you're a fool, and I've seen nothing to suggest that."

"Thanks, I think. I'll try to see Lamar before he leaves the hospital, but in case I don't, make sure I know how to find you."

"You can count on that. Like I told you, you're family now," she said, giving his hand a squeeze. "And I never lose track of family, not for long, anyway."

Ryan left the shelter feeling blessed. Only a few short weeks ago he'd been satisfied with a handful of friends and a ton of acquaintances. Now he seemed to be collecting families who were determined to draw him in. Maybe if his own family rejected him for a second time, it wouldn't be quite so painful.

Now that the decision to find his biological family had been made, Ryan was anxious to get started. Unfortunately, he had no idea where to begin. He had no clue how to conduct a search for people missing for so many years. Hiring a private eye seemed like the best option, but the prospect of sharing the story with a stranger was painful. Turning to Jack Reilly once again made it easier.

To Ryan's surprise, telling the whole sad tale to Jack turned out to hurt less than it had when he'd told it to Maggie, or even to Letitia. Jack was a professional. He was used to listening without comment, and he'd probably heard far more sordid tales than the one Ryan had to tell.

Throughout the conversation, the investigator was completely matter-of-fact, taking notes and asking questions about facts and places, not about emotions.

When Jack had everything he needed, Ryan said, "One last thing—don't say anything about this to Maggie, okay?"

"You're the client," Jack said readily. "Anything you tell me is strictly confidential."

Ryan was relieved. He didn't want her to know until he had something solid to report. Besides, there was still the very real chance that even once he'd found his parents or siblings, he wouldn't be able to confront them. Why get Maggie's hopes up, only to back out?

"How long is this likely to take?" he asked Jack.

"Hard to say. The trail's been cold for a long time. Since you were all fairly young when you went into foster care, it's possible that the youngest boys were adopted. Their names could have been changed. If that happened and the records are sealed, it'll take a miracle to find them."

"And my parents?"

"Easier, I'd say, depending on where they ran off to. I'll have a better idea once I've run a few simple checks on credit reports, that kind of thing. As soon as I know anything, I'll let you know." He studied Ryan curiously. "It's been a lot of years. Is there some reason you're in a rush all of a sudden?"

"I'm not in a rush," Ryan said. "Not exactly."

But until he'd found these missing pieces to the past, he couldn't begin to think about the future with Maggie that he'd begun to yearn for.

Chapter Thirteen

Something was up with Ryan. He was edgy and distracted, and he seemed to be spending a lot of time huddled in a booth with Jack Reilly. Whenever Maggie approached, they both fell silent. It was getting on her nerves.

She was behind the bar taking inventory, something Ryan had grudgingly allowed her to do, when he came back after one of those secret talks. She saw the evident frustration in his eyes and decided to confront him.

"Okay, that's it," she said, putting down the legal pad and pen she'd been using to take notes. She scowled at him. "What is going on?"

Ryan stared at her blankly. It was a pretty good act. Even she could admit that. He looked as if he had no idea at all what she was talking about.

"You and Jack," she said, to clarify things. "What's up with all the whispering?"

"It's about a case he's working on."

"Why can he talk to *you* about it?" she asked, not buying it for a minute, "yet the two of you clam up whenever I come around."

"It's nothing for you to worry about," Ryan said dismissively, picking up the legal pad and scanning her notes. "How's our supply of Irish whisky?"

Maggie frowned at the deliberate evasiveness.

"We have an entire case, which you should know, since you ordered it day before yesterday."

He gave her a sheepish grin. "So I did." He stepped closer. "Must be you. You have a way of making me forget everything except my name." He tucked a finger under her chin and kissed her thoroughly. "Now that's something I've been waiting to do ever since you walked through the door tonight."

Her gaze narrowed at the touch of blarney in his voice. "Ryan Devaney, you're keeping something from me," she accused. "And you're being patronizing about it, as well. Just so you know, I don't like it."

"Is that so?" he asked, still not taking her nearly seriously enough. "I thought you were a woman who was fond of secrets."

"I'm a woman who is fond of *unraveling* secrets. There's a difference. I don't like things being *kept* from me."

"Is it not possible that some things don't concern you?" he inquired.

"Of course it's possible," she retorted impatiently. "But something tells me that's not the case right now."

He beckoned her closer. "If you were to put aside all those doubts and questions, I could close up now and we could go upstairs."

"You shouldn't use sex as a distraction," she chided, but her mood was definitely shifting.

Maybe she didn't have to have answers to all those burning questions just yet. Tomorrow might be soon enough. "Though if it were a promise of outrageously wicked sex you were making, I could be persuaded to go along with it."

He leaned down and whispered in her ear. His husky voice and the promise of something absolutely sinful shot the last of her resolve to smithereens. When he was in this kind of dangerous mood, he was practically irresistible.

"Lock the door," she said, her voice breathless.

His expression turned smug. "You're a surprisingly predictable woman at times, Maggie O'Brien."

Maggie glowered at him. "Not a compliment," she warned.

He didn't seem disturbed. "There are other times, though—and far more of them, I might add—when you're so unpredictable you make a man's head spin."

Pleased by that assessment, she kissed him. "Much better. Which am I tonight?"

He gave her a considering look. "Now that remains to be seen, doesn't it?"

Heat shot through her at the speculative gleam in his eyes. She headed for the stairs. "If you dawdle over closing up, I'll have to come down here and have my way with you on the bar."

He laughed. "You've been begging to do that since the first night we made love. One of these nights I'll have to accommodate you, though it seems to me that a bed is a more practical, comfortable choice."

"Sometimes the thrill of accepting a dare offsets whatever discomfort is involved," she teased. "But tonight the bed will do."

In fact, just about any place where she could feel Ryan's arms around her and his body joined with hers was a magical place indeed. And with each and every day that passed, Maggie was growing more and more confident that Ryan felt the same.

If only there weren't this faint shadow threatening her happiness.

Two days later Maggie looked up from behind the bar and spotted her entire family coming through the door. Her mother shot her a rueful look as they made their way to the biggest table in the room. Maggie sighed. She might not be able to kick them right back out, but she could certainly avoid them, at least for a while. She turned to Maureen.

"That crowd that just came in," she said, nodding in her family's direction. "They belong to me, but I think I'll give you the pleasure of waiting on them. I have the feeling they're here on a mission."

"What sort of mission?" Maureen inquired curiously.

"I haven't been home for a few days now."

Maureen's gaze shot to Ryan, who was just emerging from the kitchen. "I see. How lovely!"

"I imagine that depends on your point of view," Maggie said, eyeing her family warily. "Go and keep them occupied, while I warn Ryan."

Maureen laughed. "Judging from that panicked look in his eyes, he doesn't need warning," she said, but she took her order pad and made her way to the table.

Ryan joined Maggie behind the bar. "Exactly how dire is this situation?" he asked, his gaze locked worriedly on the O'Brien entourage.

"I imagine that depends," she said. "If you can cope with a few questions about your intentions, and assuming they're honorable enough, I imagine the weapons will remain sheathed."

Ryan swallowed hard. "Well now, there's an incentive to race over to St. Mary's and pray. Where's Father Francis when I need him? They'd never attack with a priest beside me."

"Don't count on it," Maggie said. "There is one other choice. I could go over there, announce that I'm the happiest I've been in years, and tell them if they do one single thing to mess that up, I'll never forgive them."

Ryan nodded. "I like that choice."

"Of course you do," she said. "It keeps you out of harm's way."

"True enough," he admitted. "But before you

go, mind telling me something? Is it true what you just said?"

"What?"

"That you're happy?"

She regarded him with shock. "How could you possibly question that?"

He shrugged. "It's a habit, I guess." Avoiding her gaze, he added, "Whenever something seems too good to be true, I'm always waiting for it to be snatched away."

His tone was so bleak and there was such sadness behind the words that Maggie made a decision. She latched on to his hand with a firm grip. "You're coming with me," she said, as she dragged him toward the table.

When she reached her family, she pinned her gaze on her mother. "I imagine you came tonight to hear the band," she said. "It's a wonderful group just over from Dublin."

"The music be damned," John said, scowling at Ryan. "We came because you've all but vanished from the house. We wanted to see if you were all right."

"And why wouldn't I be?" Maggie inquired. "I'm with Ryan, aren't I?"

"That's what we've been worrying about," Matt said. "Do you really know what you're doing? Has he made any promises?" His gaze was locked on Ryan, even though he'd addressed the questions to her.

Maggie rolled her eyes at the growling note of protectiveness in his voice. "I haven't asked for any," she said. "And what goes on between Ryan and me is our business. He makes me happy. That's all that should concern any of you."

Ryan met John's gaze, then Matt's. "I can understand your concern," he said. "If I had a sister like Maggie, I'd want to do everything in my power to keep her from getting hurt, too."

"So?" John pushed.

"I'm not going to hurt her," Ryan said. "Not intentionally, anyway."

When her brothers seemed about to leap on the opening he'd left himself, Maggie's mother interceded. "That's good enough for me," she said cheerfully. "Shouldn't you back off now, Matthew? John?" It was quite clearly not a request but an order.

"I haven't heard a word about marriage," John said, defying her.

Ryan looked him in the eye. "And you're not the one I'd be proposing to, either."

Katie and Colleen smothered laughter at John's look of indignation.

"I'd say he has you there," Matt said, relenting a little. He looked back at Ryan. "Just know that we're keeping an eye on things."

"That's as it should be," Ryan agreed, accepting the warning.

Maggie's father had kept silent through the entire exchange, but he gave a nod of satisfaction now. "That's that, then. I'll have a glass of your finest ale. Can you join us, lad?"

"I'm needed at the bar just now, but I'll be back," Ryan promised. "Maggie, why don't you join your family for dinner? It's on the house."

"You cannot be giving away dinner to a crowd like this," she retorted, thinking of the dent it would make in his bottom line for the night. "What kind of business practice is that? Next thing you know, all your regulars will be coming in with their families and asking for the same deal you gave the O'Briens."

Her brothers hooted. "Now isn't that what every man needs, a woman with a head for business standing beside him?" John said.

"But at the moment, it is my business," Ryan said, his gaze clashing with hers in a test of wills with which she was increasingly familiar. "And I'm of a mind to buy dinner for your family."

"Then we'll be grateful for it," her mother said, giving Maggie a pointed look. "Won't we, Maggie?"

Maggie uttered a sigh of resignation and pulled up a chair beside her mother. She knew better than they exactly what Ryan was doing. He was hoping to pacify the wolves with a hearty meal . . . and just in case it didn't work, he was throwing her to them.

• • •

Keeping Maggie from learning the truth about his meetings with Jack Reilly was getting to be increasingly difficult for Ryan. When the P.I. came to him a few days later with the news that he had a lead on Ryan's brother Sean, Ryan was relieved on several levels. If nothing else, it meant he finally had something concrete to share with Maggie.

"What did you find out?" he asked the detective as an image of his dark-haired brother came to mind. "Where is he? Is he okay?"

"He's right here in Boston, working as a firefighter," Jack told him. "The trail led to his last foster family, but I had the devil's own time getting a word out of them. They were afraid that you'd just be stirring up bad memories. Finally I convinced them to contact him. I gave them my number, and he called earlier today."

"And?"

"He wants to see you. Here's the address and the phone number. The number's unlisted, so don't lose track of it."

"Did you tell him anything about me?"

Jack shook his head. "I wasn't sure if you wanted me to, so I just said you'd been anxious to find him and that I was sure you'd be in touch soon."

Ryan sighed. So, this was it? he thought, staring at the piece of paper with Sean's address. It was only a couple of miles away. It was hard to imagine, but they could have passed on the street a thousand times and not even known it.

"You going to call him now?" Jack asked.

Ryan shook his head. "I need to tell someone first."

"Maggie?"

"Yes."

"Well, I'll leave you to it, then. Do you want me to keep looking for the others?"

No matter how this reunion went, Ryan knew he needed to find the rest of them now. He had to play this out to the end. "Of course."

"I'll be in touch, then." Jack glanced toward the door and smiled. "And here comes Maggie now. Just in time, I'd say."

He waved to Maggie, then took off. Maggie's gaze followed him from the bar before she came over and joined Ryan. "Another of those top-secret meetings? It must be quite a case he's handling."

Ryan slipped the piece of paper in his pocket. Despite Jack's advice, he wasn't ready to share the news yet. He needed to absorb it.

"Where have you been off to?" he asked, deliberately ignoring her question.

She regarded him with disappointment, but let the matter drop. "I went to see Lamar," she said.

"How is he?"

"Getting stronger every day. He wants to see you."

"I'll get by there this week. Is the new apartment okay?"

"A little small, but it's clean and in a nice neighborhood. Letitia says it's a palace compared to the place where they were forced to stay before she gave up and moved to the shelter. We looked over her budget and found a way for her to put a little aside from Jamal's paycheck each week toward a down payment on a house. Once Lamar is back on his feet, she's going to look for work, too." Maggie eyed him speculatively. "I suggested she find a book of Irish recipes at the library and practice a bit, then invite us over for dinner."

Ryan shook his head. "As if Father Francis weren't bad enough, now you're going to be bringing me new employees?"

"I never said anything about you hiring her," Maggie said, her expression perfectly innocent. "But it's a great idea, don't you think? Besides, Rosita will be having her baby anytime now, so there'll be an opening in the kitchen."

"As if Rosita has done a lick of work since she came," Ryan grumbled.

"Only because Rory is a gentleman," Maggie replied.

"Okay, fine. Whatever. If Letitia needs a job, we'll work it out."

Maggie studied him with a narrowed gaze, as if she suspected his capitulation had been too easy. “Is everything okay? Is there something you’re not telling me?”

Ryan frowned at the question. “Who says I’m keeping anything from you?” he asked defensively.

“Nothing’s really changed, has it?” she asked. “You still can’t let me all the way into your life.”

He heard the unmistakable hurt in her voice. Regret washed through him, but he couldn’t make himself share the truth. Not just yet. “I’m sorry, Maggie. I’m trying, but I’m not there yet. Be patient, okay?”

She sighed heavily. “Since I’m in love with you, it seems I have no choice.”

Her easy claim of love startled him. He’d known her feelings for him were growing, but to have her admit that she actually loved him caught him off guard. Even more surprising was the fact that it didn’t terrify him. Rather, it made him want to admit that his feelings were growing deeper as well.

He took her hand in his, swallowed hard, then fumbled until he found the right words. “If it’s any consolation, I love you, too.” The admission had been easier than he’d expected, but he couldn’t help adding a quick disclaimer. “At least as much as I know how to love anyone. Can that be enough for you?”

A faint glimmer of a smile appeared on her lips. “For now,” she said, her eyes shimmering with unshed tears. “It is for now.”

• • •

Ryan must have looked at that slip of paper with Sean's address on it a dozen times a day. Each time he picked up the phone to call his brother, then settled the receiver back into its cradle. For two solid weeks that paper taunted him, as did the worried frown puckering Maggie's brow. He evaded all the questions Rory and Father Francis had about his dark mood, as well. He was driving them all away, and all because he was afraid to tell them the momentous news that he'd found one of his brothers.

At night, lying awake in bed next to a sleeping Maggie, he questioned why he was having such a difficult time with this. It didn't take long for him to figure out the answer. He was desperately afraid of how seeing Sean again might change things.

What if his brother hated him for standing by and watching him walk away with strangers that day and doing nothing? For all Ryan knew, Sean could have found their parents and discovered that Ryan's worst fear was accurate, that he had somehow driven them away. He knew it was a boy's fear, not that of a rational grown-up, but he couldn't seem to turn his back on it just the same. He'd lived with that guilt burning inside him for too many years.

Greater than the fear of all that, though, was this mounting panic that if he didn't do something, Maggie would eventually slip away. Despite her promise to give him all the time he needed, it was already happening. She was growing more reserved as he insisted on keeping his secret. The openness he prized in her was giving way to brooding silences. He couldn't let that go on or he would lose her forever. He sighed heavily.

"Ryan?" she murmured, rolling toward him. "Are you awake?"

He nodded, then realized she probably had her eyes closed. "Yes. Go back to sleep. I didn't mean to disturb you."

Instead, she propped herself on her elbow and studied him sleepily. "What's wrong?"

"I have a lot on my mind."

"Please tell me."

He hesitated, then drew in a deep breath. This was the moment he'd been waiting for, here in the dark, where she couldn't read his expression so readily.

When he didn't speak right away, she said, "Is it so hard to talk to me? There's nothing you can't say now. I want to be here for you, but I can't be if you won't let me in."

She was right and he knew it. "Okay, here it is. I've had Jack looking for my family," he said quietly.

"Really?" Maggie remarked, her voice surprisingly neutral, as if she didn't want to risk getting excited. "And?"

Relieved by her calm, accepting reaction, he went on. "He's found one of my brothers."

"Oh, my God," she murmured. "Which one?"

"Sean. He's two years younger than I am."

He felt her tears fall on his bare chest. "Oh, Ryan, that's wonderful! How long have you known?"

"A couple of weeks now."

"And you haven't said a word? Why not?"

"I'm not entirely sure why I haven't," he admitted candidly.

"Have you been to see him?"

"No. . . ."

"Why on earth not? Is he here in Boston?"

He shrugged, feeling helpless. "Only a couple of miles away, as a matter of fact. And to be honest, I don't know why I haven't called or gone to see him. He must be wondering about it, too, since Jack told him I was looking for him."

"Oh, Ryan, put yourself in his shoes," Maggie said urgently. "It must be awful waiting for a call that hasn't come. It must be a little bit like reliving what he went through after your parents took off. I'm sure all of you kept expecting to get a phone call any day."

"Oh, God," Ryan whispered, struck by her words. "I never looked at it that way. You're right, Maggie. It was months before I finally accepted the fact that they weren't calling and weren't coming back." The memory still haunted him.

How many hours had he stayed near the phone wherever he was, waiting, trying desperately not to hope when it rang, fighting tears when it wasn't for him.

"That's when I started getting in trouble," he told Maggie. "Once I knew that it didn't matter where I was, because they were never going to look for me, I didn't care if I was moved from foster home to foster home. I didn't want to get attached to any of those families, so whenever I felt myself letting down my guard, I'd do something to get sent away."

He felt Maggie's hand on his cheek.

"It must have been so awful for you," she said sympathetically. "And now you have a chance to get back something you lost. Don't wait another day. Call Sean. Go to see him."

Ryan wasn't sure he could do it alone. "Would you . . . ?" He looked into Maggie's eyes. "I want you to come with me."

To his dismay she shook her head. "Ryan, after all these years this should be private, just the two of you."

He searched his heart for the strength, but it wasn't there. Besides, having Maggie with him, since she'd been the one to encourage the search, felt right. "No, I need you to be there. If we're going to be family, that's how it should be."

She stared at him, clearly stunned by the casual

mention of a future for the two of them. "Are we? Are we going to be family?"

He was just as shocked that she hadn't known that that was what they were leading up to, that it was the reason for everything he'd done lately to deal with the past. He was desperately trying to tie up all the loose ends so he could move forward with a clear conscience.

"That's why I'm doing this," he explained. "I want to find them all, to make sure that, you know, there are no problems you ought to know about before you marry me."

"Problems?" she asked, clearly bewildered.

"Illnesses, that kind of thing," he said, avoiding her gaze.

Maggie sat straight up in bed and regarded him with unmistakable dismay. "You're looking for them to see if everyone's *healthy?*"

"Of course," he said defensively. "That's the responsible thing to do."

"And that's the only reason?" she asked, disbelief still written all over her face.

"It's important, dammit!"

"Oh, Ryan," she whispered, fresh tears tracking down her cheeks. "It shouldn't be about that."

And then, to his shock, she climbed out of bed, dragged on her clothes and left the room without so much as a glance in his direction. And somehow, despite the terrible, aching emptiness inside him, he couldn't find a single word to call her back.

Chapter Fourteen

Ryan didn't get it. He'd done what Maggie wanted. Maybe he hadn't found his whole family, but he'd found one of his brothers. That was a start, dammit! What did she want from him? If she was expecting the Devaneys to suddenly turn all warm and fuzzy like the O'Briens—well, it wasn't going to happen. There was too blasted much water under the bridge for that.

"Ryan, you've the look of a man with a lot on his mind," Father Francis said, sliding onto a stool at the bar. "Anything I can help with?"

"Not unless you can explain the way a woman's mind works," Ryan retorted.

Father Francis grinned. "Now that is a mysterious thing," he agreed. "Are we talking about any woman's mind, or is it Maggie's that has you looking as if there's a dark cloud hanging over your head?"

"Maggie's, of course."

"I notice she hasn't been coming in as regularly as she was," Father Francis said. "It's been a few days since her last visit, hasn't it?"

"Close to a week," Ryan admitted despondently.

"Have you spoken to her?"

He shook his head. What was the point of calling, when he didn't know what to say?

Father Francis looked dismayed. "Now there's your first mistake, it seems to me. Whether he's right or wrong, a man should take the first step toward making things right." He gave Ryan a canny look. "Unless, of course, you're happy with the way things are."

"No, of course not, but I don't know the first thing about smoothing this over. I have no idea what Maggie expects. She's the one who walked out." It was a disingenuous statement, and Ryan knew it. He knew precisely why Maggie was so furious. She was outraged because he cared more about making sure his family health history was problem free than he did about some phony family reunion.

Father Francis studied him intently. "She left without giving you any clue at all about why she was upset?" the priest asked doubtfully. "That doesn't sound like Maggie."

"Are you calling me a liar?" Ryan asked edgily.

"No, of course not. Have you thought of asking her to explain, then?"

"It's not that simple."

Father Francis clearly wasn't convinced. "Why, because Maggie won't be honest?"

"Of course not," Ryan said at once. "Maggie's the most honest person I know."

"Is it because she won't be able to tell you what's in her heart?"

Ryan sighed. "No."

"What then?"

"It's because I still won't be able to give her the answers she wants."

"About?"

"My family." Ryan regarded the priest helplessly. "How can I tell her I care about seeing them again, when the truth is that I don't?"

"Ah, so that's it," Father Francis said. "Have you finally decided to search for them, then? I imagine Maggie's had a hand in helping you reach that decision. Are you not comfortable with it now that you've made it? Are you considering backing down?"

"Too late for that," Ryan said wryly. "Actually, Jack Reilly's been looking for a while now. He's found one of my brothers—Sean, the one two years younger than me, which would make him about thirty now."

The old man's face lit up. "That's brilliant news. Have you seen him?"

"I can see that your expectations are the same as Maggie's," Ryan said. "You're expecting me to be overjoyed."

"And you're not?"

"I'm just looking for answers."

"What sort of answers? You do realize that if he was younger than you, Sean may not have the answers you need. Unless he's found your parents, it's unlikely he knows what went wrong."

Ryan shook his head. "That's not it at all. I want

to be sure everyone's in good health, so if Maggie and I ever decide to marry and have a family, I won't be unwittingly passing any hereditary conditions along to our children."

Father Francis sighed heavily. "I imagine this is because of Lamar," he said. "And you told this to Maggie, that your search is all about genetics?"

"Yes," Ryan admitted.

The priest gave him a pitying look. "It's a wonder she didn't take a skillet to your head. I'm thinking of it myself," he said with disgust. "You clearly know how to rob a moment of its meaning."

"If you're trying to accuse me of not being a sentimental jerk, then you're right. I'm not. This is a practical search for answers I need to have before I decide whether it's right to take the next step with Maggie."

"No," the priest said flatly. "It's a way of protecting yourself from being hurt again. You're taking no chances that your brother—or the others when you find them—might not want to be a part of your life even now."

Ryan felt the undeniable sting of truth in his words. "What if I am? Can you blame me?"

"Of course not, but life is about risks, about being open to possibilities. Have you not been happier these last weeks with Maggie than you ever have been before?"

There seemed to be little to gain by lying when

the answer was obvious. "Yes. What's your point?"

"If you'd continued to keep the door to your heart tightly shut, you'd have had none of that," Father Francis reminded him. "Life would have gone along on its nice, even keel with no ups and downs. It would have been safe. But you'd have missed all the joy Maggie has brought into your life. Wasn't that worth the risk of letting down your defenses?"

Much as Ryan wanted to protest that he'd been better off before, he knew it wasn't true. Maggie had opened up his heart, and there was no turning back.

"And you think that seeing my brothers and even my parents again could turn out as well?" he asked skeptically. "Despite the fact that I've spent all these years with bitterness and resentment churning around inside me?"

"You'll never know unless you try . . . and for the right reasons. And you'll need to be willing to let go of the bitterness and resentment and be ready to move on. Surely your brother's not the one you've been angry with. Wouldn't that be a good place to start? I'm sure he's been grappling with many of the same resentments that you have."

"Okay, you win. I'll call Sean in the morning."

"It's not about what I want or about me winning. It's about you. And is there any reason for not calling him right now?" Father Francis pushed.

Ryan frowned, but he reached for the phone.

With the priest's steady gaze on him, he dialed his brother's number. Unfortunately, it was an answering machine that picked up. Hearing his brother's voice after all these years—his deep, grown-up voice—threw Ryan. Sean sounded so much like their dad, it was uncanny and disturbing. But before he could lose his nerve, he left a message.

"Sean, this is Ryan . . . um, your brother Ryan." He considered hanging up then, but after a glance at Father Francis's expectant, encouraging expression, he plunged on. "I'd like to see you. If it's okay, I'll stop by tomorrow around ten. I have the address. If I miss you then, I'll come by another time." He searched his brain for something more, but nothing came to him. "Um, I guess that's it. Bye."

To his shock, his hand was shaking as he replaced the receiver in its cradle. Father Francis covered his hand to steady it.

"You've taken a first step, lad, the first of many."

Ryan swallowed past the lump in his throat. "I just wish to hell I knew where they were going to lead."

Maggie had been for an hour-long walk, but it hadn't done a thing to steady her nerves or calm her temper. Nor had any of the other walks she'd taken since she'd walked out of Ryan's apartment and out of his life. She'd been expecting him to call, but the phone had remained stubbornly silent. It shouldn't have surprised her. If he hadn't reached out to his family in all these years, why was she expecting him to reach out to her? Back then he'd been too young to fight for what he needed. Now he was evidently too scared.

Back at the house, half-frozen, she poured herself a cup of tea, then sat at the kitchen table, brooding over the way things were turning out. She'd been so sure that Ryan was the one, that her love could give him the strength to face his past and move on. Maybe it was impossible after what he'd been through. Maybe she'd been expecting too much once again, just as she had when she'd wanted more passion from her last relationship. Maybe her expectations simply couldn't be met, at least never all at once.

She was still thinking that over, debating whether there was more she could have done to get through to him, when her mother walked into the kitchen.

"I thought I heard you come in," Nell O'Brien said, pouring herself a cup of tea, then putting a few freshly baked shortbread cookies onto a plate before sitting down opposite Maggie.

"Uh-oh, you've brought out the cookies," Maggie teased. "You must be anticipating a serious talk."

"I am, indeed. I've waited patiently for you to tell me what happened between you and Ryan, but you haven't said a word. I've lost patience," her mother said. "And since Father Francis called a while ago with a rather cryptic message, I've concluded that it's time to get to the bottom of things."

Maggie sat up a little straighter. "Father Francis called? What did he want?"

"He said Ryan was going to try to see his brother at ten this morning. He seemed to think you'd be interested in that, that you might want to be there."

"No way," Maggie said fiercely. "I am not going to help him do this, not when he's doing it for all the wrong reasons."

"What reasons are those?" her mother asked.

"The stupid idiot thinks I'm worried about his genes," Maggie grumbled. "Can you imagine anything more ridiculous? I don't give two figs about that."

"Aren't you assuming it's all about you?" her mother asked mildly. "And isn't that a bit presumptuous?"

"I'm not assuming anything. That's what Ryan said. He said he needed to know if everyone was okay, if there were any medical skeletons in the closet, before he could contemplate a future with me."

Her mother gave her a pitying look. "And you took that at face value?"

"He said it, didn't he?" Maggie replied defensively, even as her conviction began to waver.

"Have you considered for an instant that maybe that's the only way he can let himself think?" she asked Maggie. "If he lets himself be vulnerable, if he lets himself envision being reunited with his family, what happens if he's rejected again?"

She let that image sink in before she continued. "Can you imagine what it must have been like for him to be abandoned when he was only nine? It was devastating enough to shape the rest of his life. Can't you remember how skittish he was just being in the same room with all of us, as if being around a big family scared him to death? It's only because of your persistence that he's let the walls around his heart come down at all."

As she listened to her mother's interpretation, shame flooded through Maggie. How could she not have seen that, when her mother had grasped it at once? Of course, that was it. This was a way for Ryan to cover emotions far too fragile for him to deal with.

"Go with him this morning," her mother encouraged. "Don't let him do this alone. Be there for him no matter how it turns out. He's taking a first step, Maggie. And he may say he's only doing it for you and for all sorts of practical reasons, but he's doing it for himself, as well. Whether he admits it or not, there has to have been an empty place inside him all these years.

He's about to reach out and try to mend at least some of the hurt. That must be a very scary thing to a man whose heart's been broken the way his has been. Some people never truly recover from deep childhood hurts."

"You're right," Maggie said. "I'm the one who's been an idiot. What time did Father Francis say he was going over there? Can I still make it?"

"He said Ryan had left a message saying he'd be there at ten. Here's the address. You should have just enough time, if you hurry." She smiled. "He's a good man, Maggie."

"I know that. I think I was just expecting him to be a saint." She recalled what Ryan had said to her the night they'd first met, that he wasn't the man Father Francis was likely to make him out to be. If only she'd listened then, perhaps her expectations wouldn't have been so unreasonable.

Ryan had so many qualms about going through with this meeting that he'd almost turned right around and driven back home a half dozen times. It was the prospect of facing Father Francis's disappointment—and Maggie's, assuming she ever started speaking to him again—that kept him going until he reached the street on which Sean's apartment was located.

It was in an older neighborhood, where brownstones had been converted into multifamily dwellings. It wasn't exactly shabby, but it wasn't an area that had been gentrified either. Even so, it was head and shoulders above the neighborhood they'd lived in as kids.

He spotted Sean's building, drove around the block, then found a parking space just down the street. But once he'd cut the engine, he couldn't seem to make himself leave the car. Suddenly he was awash in memories.

Because they'd been the oldest, barely two years apart, he and Sean had been best friends. Sean had been his shadow from the moment he learned to walk. He'd even insisted Ryan walk with him on his first day of school, rather than their mother, because he hadn't wanted to look like a baby. They'd played baseball together at the small park down the street. Ryan had taught him to ride the secondhand bike he'd managed to buy from a church thrift store with the pocket change he'd earned by helping elderly neighbors carry their groceries or wash their cars.

None of that had changed when Michael came along. Ryan and Sean had welcomed their new brother, waiting impatiently until he was old enough to go with them everywhere. They were brothers, and that's what brothers did.

But when the twins were born, everything changed. They were fussier babies, and the mere fact that there were two of them in an increasingly crowded apartment added to the tension. Tempers flared more often. Ryan couldn't count the number of evenings he and Sean had fled from the apartment in tears because of the shouting between his parents. Michael, too little to follow, had huddled in his bed and cried just as hard as the babies.

In retrospect, he probably shouldn't have been surprised when their family collapsed under the weight of all that stress. But coming home after school to an empty apartment, standing inside the deserted rooms with Sean's hand tucked in his, had been a shock.

They'd been there only moments when the neighbor caring for Michael came in with him in tow, her face pale and tears welling up in her eyes. She'd still been trying to explain that their parents had disappeared with the twins when the social worker arrived to take over.

They'd gone to an emergency foster care home together that first night. Michael had finally cried himself out and fallen asleep, but Ryan and Sean had huddled together in bed, whispering, trying to make sense of what had happened, trying desperately not to be afraid.

They hadn't been allowed to go back to their old school, which was across town. Instead, while the social worker tried to locate their parents, they had waited, terrified to ask what would happen if their parents weren't found.

The memory of what happened next was burned forever into Ryan's brain. The social worker had lined them all up on the sofa in the foster family's living room and explained that for now they were going to be wards of the state, that they would be going to new families who would care for them until all the legal issues could be resolved.

Ryan had faced her defiantly. "We're staying together, though, right?"

"I'm sorry," she said with sympathy, "but no. We don't have a home that can take all three of you."

Sean had stood up then, his arms across his chest. "Then I'm not going," he said. "I want to be with my brothers."

"Me, too," Michael had whispered, his eyes filling with tears, his hand tucked in Ryan's.

"I wish that were possible," she replied, her gaze on Ryan. "It will be okay. We'll look for a place where you can stay together, but it may not be for a while."

Ryan had heard the finality in her tone and known it was useless to argue. Still, with Sean's gaze on him, he'd felt as if he had to try. "You don't understand. Sean and me need to look out for Michael. He's still little and he's our responsibility." It was a lesson that had been ingrained in them from the first time their brother had left the house with them to play. They were to protect him against any eventuality, but they'd never envisioned anything like this.

“I’m sorry,” she said. “Sean and Michael will be coming with me now. You’ll stay here tonight. I’ll have a new family ready for you tomorrow.” She’d turned to his brothers and spoken briskly. “Get your things, boys.”

“No,” Sean said, still defiant.

Ryan had looked into the woman’s unrelenting gaze and known it was over. “You don’t have a choice, Sean,” he’d said, defeated. “We have to do what she says.”

Ryan would never forget the look of betrayal in Sean’s eyes as he left. Ryan had watched through the living room window as they drove away, but Sean had never looked back. All of his attention had been focused on Michael, who was sobbing his eyes out.

Ryan hadn’t cried that night or the next, when he’d been transferred to his first official foster home. For weeks he’d asked about his brothers, but the replies had been evasive, and eventually he’d given up. Even at nine he’d known that he was no match for a system run by adults. He’d fought back the only way he knew how—by stirring up trouble everywhere he went.

It had been a childish form of retaliation against people who’d only wanted to help. He could see that now, but back then it had become a way of life, his only way of lashing back.

Now, staring up at Sean’s apartment, he sighed. How could Sean possibly forgive him when he couldn't forgive himself for not finding his brothers years ago, for not reuniting them? It didn't matter that he'd only been nine. As the years passed, he could have found a way.

Maybe Sean hadn't forgiven him. Maybe the reason Sean had passed along his address was simply because he wanted an opportunity to vent years of pent-up rage. Ryan thought he might even welcome such a reaction. It couldn't possibly be worse than the anger he'd directed inward all these years.

There was only one way to find out how Sean felt, though. He had to cross the street, walk up the stairs and knock on his door. And he'd do just that . . . any minute now.

Maggie clutched the address of the apartment across town where Ryan was going to meet his brother. She drove there with her heart in her throat. When she found the block, even though it was after ten o'clock, she spotted Ryan sitting in his car, his shoulders slumped, his gaze locked on the building where his brother lived.

She crossed the street and tapped on his window. "Want some company?"

He rolled the window down, even as he shook his head. "Too late."

"You've already seen him?"

"Nope. I've decided this is a bad idea."

Maggie walked around to the passenger side

and slid in. “You’ll never forgive yourself if you get this close and don’t follow through.”

“I’m used to it. There are a lot of things I’ve never forgiven myself for.”

“Such as?”

“I should have stopped them from leaving.”

“Who? Your parents?” she asked incredulously. “You think you could have changed their minds?”

“I should have tried.”

“Did you even know what they were planning?”

“No.”

“Well then, how were you supposed to stop it?”

“I was the oldest. I should have figured out what was going on.”

“You were nine!”

He turned a bleak expression on her. “What if Sean can’t forgive me?”

“First you have to give him a chance. If he doesn’t, then at least you’ve tried.”

He studied her face, then finally drew in a ragged breath, and nodded. “Okay, let’s do it.”

The walk up that sidewalk and into the building was the longest Maggie had ever taken, because Ryan’s tension was palpable. When he knocked on the door, it was opened by a man who was almost his spitting image. His hair was shorter. He didn’t have the scar on his mouth. But there was no mistaking the fact that these two men were brothers.

Maggie held her breath as they stared at each

other, sizing each other up, maintaining a reserve that no brothers should ever feel.

"Sean?"

The younger man nodded.

Ryan swallowed hard, then said in a voice barely above a whisper. "I'm Ryan. Your brother."

For what seemed like an eternity, Sean didn't reply, but finally, when Maggie was about to give up hope, he opened his arms. "Ah, man, what the hell took you so long?"

Chapter Fifteen

Ryan clung to his brother, fighting tears of relief and surprising joy. Never in a million years had he expected to feel this way. He'd anticipated looking into the face of a stranger, feeling no more than a faint twinge of recognition perhaps. Instead, it was as if they'd never been apart, as if on some level the deep connection between them as children had never been broken.

Finally Ryan stood back and surveyed his brother, noting that Sean's hair was shorter but still had a defiant tendency to curl, just as his did. The eyes were the same as well, though perhaps the blue was a shade deeper.

"I guess you've never been in my pub after all," he said at last. "I'd have known you anywhere. You look like Dad."

"I look like *you,*" Sean said, making no attempt at all to hide his bitterness at the mention of their father. "Come on in. The place isn't fancy, but it's clean—though only because I've been straightening up ever since I got your message last night." He shrugged. "Couldn't sleep."

Ryan grinned. "I didn't get much myself."

"That must be why you've been sitting out there in your car for the past half hour," Sean said with a touch of wit as wry as Ryan's. "Did you fall asleep?"

"You knew I was there?" Ryan asked, startled.

"I've been watching out the window all morning. I saw you drive up."

"Why didn't you come out?"

"Stubbornness mainly," Sean admitted. "I was still mad at you."

"Past tense?" Ryan asked.

Sean turned his gaze to Maggie, then said, "Only if you introduce me to this beautiful woman who's been waiting patiently for you to remember her."

Ryan reached out and clasped Maggie's hand, pulling her forward. "Sean, this is Maggie O'Brien. She's the reason I'm here."

Sean started to shake her hand, then pulled her into a hug instead. "Thank you. I owe you for turning up and getting him out of that car."

"It went beyond that," Ryan told him. "But, yes, she did persuade me I'd come too far to turn back this morning."

"I'm so glad it worked out," Maggie said, swiping at a tear tracking down her cheek. "I should let you two spend some time alone. You have a lot of catching up to do."

"No," Ryan said at once. "Please stay." He wanted her there as a buffer . . . and because she deserved to be a part of this reunion.

She glanced from him to Sean. "Is that okay with you?"

"Absolutely. I've made a huge pot of coffee.

And I bought a pecan coffee cake from the bakery down the street," he said.

Ryan felt a sharp stab of pain. "Pecan coffee cake was Mom's favorite," he said, suddenly remembering.

Sean nodded. "She baked one for every special occasion—our birthdays, Christmas morning, Easter."

Ryan sighed. "You still think about that, too?"

"I guess so. I've been buying coffee cakes all these years."

He led the way into the kitchen, then handed a knife to Ryan. "You cut the cake. I'll pour the coffee. Maggie, have a seat."

For the next hour Ryan and Sean exchanged news about their lives. When Ryan described his pub, Sean glanced at Maggie. "And that's where the two of you met?"

She nodded and told about her flat tire on Thanksgiving.

"Now she's trying to take over the place and run my life," Ryan said.

Sean laughed. "You don't sound as if you object all that strenuously."

"I'm getting used to the idea," Ryan admitted, giving her hand a squeeze.

"On that note I think I really will leave," Maggie said. "You two stay right here. I can find my way out."

Ryan's gaze caught hers. "Will you be at the pub later?"

Maggie smiled. "Of course. Haven't you just said I'm taking over? Guess that means I can finally start fiddling with your financial records."

"Don't even think about it," Ryan said with feigned ferocity.

"You don't scare me," she retorted over her shoulder.

"Hey, Maggie," he called. When she stepped back into the kitchen, he met her gaze. "I'm glad you came this morning."

"Any time you need me, chances are I'll be around somewhere."

After she'd gone, Ryan saw his brother studying him.

"So, this thing with you and Maggie is serious?" Sean asked.

"As serious as I've ever allowed any relationship to be. I love her."

"Marriage?"

"It's looking that way," he admitted.

"I'm really glad for you. She seems like a great woman."

"You have no idea," Ryan said. "What about you? Anybody serious in your life?"

"Afraid not. I have *issues,* according to the women I've dated."

Ryan laughed. "Yeah, join the club. Maggie didn't seem to care. She badgered me until the issues didn't seem so damned important anymore. You'll find someone like that one of these days.

Start dropping by the pub. I've got some regulars there who'd probably swoon at the sight of you."

"I'm not interested in your rejects," Sean retorted, grinning. "I can find my own women. I just can't keep 'em." His expression suddenly sobered. "Have you ever looked for the others?"

"Not until now. You?"

Sean shook his head. "I didn't think I ever wanted to see any of you again till I heard your voice. Michael's the one I really wonder about. He was so scared the last time I saw him, and he couldn't stop crying. He kept trying to run back to me, but they wouldn't let him. It's an image I've never been able to shake. All these years I kept praying that he adapted, maybe even ended up with an adoptive family. He was still so little, I told myself that he'd forget all about us. Do you think he did?"

"I try not to think about it," Ryan said tightly.

"Maybe we should think about it," Sean said. "I know how I've felt all this time, as if I was waiting and waiting for someone to come looking for me and pretending it didn't matter when no one did."

Ryan was filled with that familiar sense of overwhelming guilt. "I'm sorry, Sean. It should have been me. I should have looked a long time ago."

His brother shook his head. "No, man, Mom and Dad are the ones who should have looked. Hell, they never should have left in the first place. What were they thinking?"

"I have no idea, and to be perfectly honest, I don't give a damn."

Sean blinked at the vehement response. "Really? You honestly don't care why they did what they did?"

"The point is, they did it. The reason hardly matters."

Sean let the matter drop. A grin tugged at his lips. "I still can't believe you have your own pub and it's only a couple of miles from here."

"We have great Irish music on Fridays and Saturdays. Will you come by this weekend?"

"Will your Maggie be around to keep me company?" he asked.

"You heard her. She'll likely be there, but don't be getting any ideas about her."

"I didn't see a ring on her finger," Sean teased.

Ryan chuckled. "You always did want whatever I had, and most of the time I let you have it. Not this time. Stay away from Maggie."

"I imagine you have to give that warning to a lot of men."

"More than you can imagine," Ryan agreed.

"Then marry her and end the problem," Sean encouraged. "I saw the love shining in her eyes earlier. I don't think you'll get any argument from her."

Ryan thought of his intention to find the rest of his family and reassure himself that there were no hidden health risks. "One of these days I will," he said.

"Don't wait too long," Sean warned him. "One of the things I've learned as a firefighter is just how short life can be. It's not something to be wasted."

"Look at you," Ryan teased, "giving advice to your big brother."

"I was always the smart one," Sean retorted.

"Yeah, right. The truth is, Michael was smarter than both of us."

Sean sighed. "He was, wasn't he? Remember how he used to plan strategies for winning whenever we played war games? He was only four, and a runt at that, but he was the only kid I ever knew who could maneuver us into a trap in the blink of an eye, even when we were watching out for it." He looked at Ryan. "Is your detective looking for him?"

Ryan nodded. "No luck so far." Reluctantly he glanced at the clock and realized that he needed to get back. The pub would be opening soon. Besides, he needed to get away and spend a little time absorbing the miraculous way this morning had gone. "I need to get to work. You'll come by soon, though, right?"

"I'm working this weekend, but next Friday for sure. I want to hear that Irish band you've been bragging about. I haven't heard a really good rendition of 'Danny Boy' since Dad used to sing it in the shower."

Ryan grinned despite himself. "He did like to sing, didn't he? And he had a voice that could make people weep, it was so beautiful." He regarded Sean with surprise. "You know, I think that's the first time I've thought of him in years without a lot of anger welling up inside me."

"I got tired of hating him years ago," Sean admitted. "But I never could bring myself to look for him, or any of the rest of you. Probably stubbornness as much as anything. I'm glad you took the initiative. One of these days that detective of yours will come through."

"Let's just pray we don't regret it," Ryan said.

"How could we? It's turned out pretty good so far, hasn't it?"

Ryan drew his brother into a hug. "Yeah, better than good, in fact."

Maggie kept glancing at the door of the pub, hoping that Ryan would appear. When the time came to open and he still wasn't back, she consulted with Rory and Maureen, and they insisted on opening without him.

"I suppose you're right," she said, but it didn't feel right.

It was dinnertime and the pub was hopping when Ryan finally walked through the door. He didn't seem the least bit surprised to see that everything was running as smoothly as usual. He simply took his place behind the bar.

As relieved as Maggie was, she still wanted to smack him for worrying her. The first chance she had, she swung by and announced, “I have a few choice words for you, mister.”

To her surprise he grinned. “Are any of them ‘I love you’?”

“That’s at the end of the list,” she said.

He sighed dramatically. “Then, you might as well start now, so we can get to the end.”

“I would, but in case you haven’t noticed, the place is packed. I have customers who are already wondering where I am with their drinks.”

He gave her a wry look. “Then you might be wanting to give me their order.”

Maggie frowned and handed it over, tapping her foot impatiently while he filled it. Eventually he slid the tray toward her, then tucked his finger beneath her chin. “Thank you for worrying about me.”

“Who said anything about worrying?” she grumbled.

“I might not have much experience with it, but I do recognize it,” he said. “I’m sorry I was late. I needed to think.”

“That’s all?”

“That’s all. As you can see, I did not run my car in a ditch. There’s not a scratch on me.”

“And your cell phone? Is the battery on that dead?”

“I ought to say it is,” he said, his gaze locked

with hers, "but I won't lie to you, Maggie. Not ever."

She gave a curt nod. "That's something, then."

She hurried away with the drinks, not because the customers were truly likely to be impatient, but because she didn't want him to see just how happy his explanation had made her. He needed to sweat a little longer for making her worry herself sick. He needed to understand that what he did—or didn't do—mattered to her.

It was hours before they had another free minute. Maggie's feet and back were aching from hauling the heavy trays around all evening, but it was a good kind of exhaustion, the kind that came from doing satisfying work.

She was just about to collapse into a chair and put her feet up, when Rory emerged from the kitchen, his face ashen.

"Um, you guys," he said in a choked voice, "I think Rosita's having the baby."

"Now? In the *kitchen?*" Juan asked, racing for the door.

Maggie took one look at Rory's panicked expression and stood up. "Sit before you faint." She pushed him onto a chair.

He gave her a pained look and popped right back up. "I'm not going to faint. And nobody has time to sit. She's in labor, and I do not want that baby born in my kitchen. Is that clear?"

Ryan patted him on the back. "Nobody's going

to have a baby here," he said. "I've already called for an ambulance. Maggie, why don't you go in there and make sure Rosita's okay?"

She frowned at him. "Sure, when it comes to babies, you big, strong men want to leave it all up to us," she grumbled, but she headed for the kitchen.

She found Rosita on the floor, clutching her stomach, her face contorted as another contraction washed over her. "How far apart are the contractions?" Maggie asked.

"Very fast," Juan answered, clutching Rosita's hand and looking dazed. He slipped into Spanish, then caught himself. "This is the second one since I've come in here."

Maggie swallowed hard. That meant they had to be less than two minutes apart. Unless the paramedics arrived in record time, they were going to be delivering the baby here, after all. She knelt beside Rosita and took her other hand. Forcing a reassuring note into her voice, she said, "Don't worry. It's going to be okay." She looked at Juan. "Tell Rory to get in here to boil some water. Tell Ryan to bring down all the towels he has upstairs."

Within a minute the kitchen was bustling with activity. The last customers had been told to send the paramedics in the instant they arrived, but by the time that happened, Rosita's baby—a boy with a full head of dark hair—was already slipping into Maggie's hands.

"Oh, my. Look how beautiful he is," she whispered, her eyes filling with tears as she handed him to the emergency medical technician, who made quick work of getting a lusty wail from him. She felt Ryan's arm slide around her waist.

"Is everything okay?" she asked the EMT.

"Looks fine to me," he said, grinning at her. "You might want to consider a new career."

"I don't think so," she said shakily, then looked at Ryan. "The only births I want to handle from here on out will be my own kids."

Her words brought a surprising smile to his lips. "We'll have to talk about that when things settle down," he said.

It didn't take long for the paramedics to whisk Rosita and Juan off to the hospital.

"I need a drink," Rory announced, his color finally returning.

"Buy one for everyone out there," Ryan told him, his gaze on Maggie.

"Where are you going?" Rory asked.

"Upstairs. Maggie and I have things to talk about."

Maggie felt her heart flutter at the heat in his gaze, but she shook her head. "Not before we toast the baby," she insisted.

He looked disappointed. "One drink, then."

She grinned. "I think a sip will do."

He laughed. "That's much better. By all means, let's have a toast to the baby."

Maggie looked into his eyes. "And to all the babies to come around here."

Rory frowned at that. "Watch your tongue, woman. There are confirmed bachelors in the room."

Ryan grinned at him. "Only one I can see."

A huge grin spread across Rory's face. "Well, isn't that lovely, then? Congratulations, Ryan, me lad."

"Hold it," Maggie interrupted. "Has anyone heard me say yes yet?"

"Now that you mention it, I haven't even heard a proper question," Rory said.

"Some things are meant to be done in private," Ryan retorted. "And in their own good time."

Maggie promptly lifted her glass. "Here's to the baby," she said, taking a quick swallow of her drink before setting it on the bar and heading for the stairs.

"Seems a bit anxious," Rory noted as she left.

She turned and winked at him. "This night's been a long time coming."

"It's been a long day. You must be exhausted," Ryan said when he joined Maggie upstairs.

"Ryan Devaney, don't think you're getting out of making good on your promise downstairs by turning all sweet and concerned. I'm not so tired that I can't listen to what you have on your mind."

From the moment he'd seen Sean that morning, Ryan had felt as if he'd discovered a piece of himself. He'd also realized that the only way to make himself completely whole and give Maggie the kind of man she deserved was to go all the way and find the rest of the family. He hadn't planned on officially proposing to her until he'd taken care of all that. But the way events had unfolded tonight had pretty much turned that plan on its ear. That didn't mean they had to rush into marriage, though.

"Shall I make a pretty speech, then?" he teased her. "Or do you know what's on my mind?"

"I think I know," she said, sitting there with her hands folded primly in her lap. "But I want all the pretty words."

"You know I love you," he began.

"I've had an inkling about that for some time," she agreed.

He regarded her sternly. "Do you intend to keep interrupting? If so, I may never get through this."

"Sorry," she said without much evidence of remorse.

"You're the most amazing, exasperating woman I've ever met. You're beautiful and strong and intelligent . . . and before you say it, I know I put that backward. It's because I get all tongue-tied just looking at you."

"Ryan Devaney, you've never been tongue-tied a day in your life," she said.

"I am now," he insisted. "I'm terrified I won't find the right words to convince you to spend the rest of your life with me."

She rested her hand against his cheek. "Any words will do," she told him quietly.

"Okay, then," he said, feeling an irresistible urge to make her laugh before things got too serious. "Will you marry me and keep the books for the pub for the rest of our days?"

As he'd anticipated, she began to chuckle. "So it's a bookkeeper you're really after, not a wife?"

He cupped her face in his hands and looked deep into her eyes. "I'm not sure I know what to do to keep a wife happy," he said with total honesty.

"I don't know about any other wife," Maggie said, regarding him seriously. "But all you need to do with me is love me for the rest of our lives."

"That I can promise you," he said.

She held out her hand. "It's a deal, then."

This time Ryan was the one laughing. "No, you don't, Maggie O'Brien. This is the sort of deal that can only be sealed with a kiss." He grinned at her. "And perhaps a bit more."

Hours later, when the deal was well and truly sealed, and Maggie's warm body was curved against his, he sighed with a feeling of pure contentment.

"Now all that's left is finding the rest of my family, and then we can plan our wedding," he murmured against her hair.

She shot up and stared at him, looking as if he'd announced a delay in the arrival of Christmas or any other cherished holiday. "You want to find them first?"

"Well, of course. Don't you want that, too?"

"Absolutely not," she said fiercely. "Don't get me wrong. I want you to locate each and every one of them for your sake, but that could take a long time, and I'm not waiting."

Ryan's heart sank. "You won't wait for me?"

"I won't wait to get married," she corrected. "Then we'll find the rest of your family together."

He stared at her. "You're asking me to marry you now?"

"Actually, I'm insisting on it. The sooner the better."

He grinned, but she noticed he wasn't arguing.

"Pushy woman, aren't you?" he teased.

"When I have to be," she confirmed with evident pride.

He pulled her back into his arms. "You're really sure you're willing to take me on without knowing everything there is to know about me?"

"I already know all the important stuff," she insisted. "For instance, you're a great kisser."

He regarded her with amusement. "Am I really?"

"Really great," she confirmed. "And a fantastic lover."

"You think so?"

She hesitated. "Come to think of it, I do have a couple of nagging little doubts. They could probably be wiped right out if you were to take me downstairs and make love to me there."

He laughed. "You're really not going to be happy till I make love to you on top of the bar, are you?"

"Try it and let's see," she dared him. "I'm pretty sure I'll be ecstatic."

He called downstairs to make absolutely certain that everyone had cleared out, then carried Maggie downstairs and did his absolute best to see that she was every bit as ecstatic as she'd been anticipating all these months.

When he held her afterward, he promised to keep right on making her happy for the rest of their lives.

"If you don't, my brothers will beat you up," she warned.

Ryan thought of the way Sean had taken an instant liking to Maggie. "If I don't, *my* brother will beat me up."

"Then I guess you're highly motivated," she teased, deliberately wiggling her hips beneath him.

"Highly motivated," he agreed, right before he set out to show her just how motivated it was possible for a man to be.

Epilogue

Despite Maggie's initial insistence on marrying before Ryan found the rest of his family, she was finally persuaded by her mother to at least wait until fall to give them time to plan a proper, lavish ceremony befitting the oldest O'Brien daughter.

"In fact," Nell had said with a sly gleam in her eye, "if you want to teach Ryan a bit more about romance, a wedding on the anniversary of your first meeting would certainly be a good way to start."

Maggie had been convinced, especially since it meant that the Thanksgiving season would mean something special to Ryan and possibly even chip away at his general hatred of holidays.

Besides, a fall color palette for the bridesmaids' dresses had made her sisters happy. With the trademark O'Brien auburn hair, they all looked fabulous in shades of bronze and gold velvet.

Maggie's dress, a heavy white satin sheath with simple pearl trim at the low neckline and a dip in back, was far more elegant and sophisticated than she'd originally envisioned, but she'd fallen in love with it the instant she'd seen it. She made a slow turn in front of the dressing room mirror, still not quite believing that her wedding day was finally here after a wait that had seemed to last an eternity. In less than an hour she would be Mrs. Ryan Devaney.

When she made one last turn, she met her mother's gaze and saw that Nell O'Brien was trying valiantly to smile through her tears.

"Mom, are you okay?"

"You're just so beautiful. They say every bride is radiant, but I swear I don't think I've ever seen one who glowed with happiness as you do right this minute."

"That's because Ryan makes me very happy."

Her mother smoothed an errant curl back into Maggie's upswept hairstyle. "He's a complicated man, your Ryan. That won't change just because he's been convinced to make a commitment to you."

"I know that. I don't think he'll ever truly be at peace until he finds the rest of his family."

"How's that search going? Anything new?"

Maggie shook her head, sharing in Ryan's frustration. Jack was concentrating on finding Michael at the moment, and he'd run into one brick wall after another.

"Ryan and Sean are ready to give up looking for their brother, Michael, but I've been pushing them to continue. I keep imagining that little boy they've described sobbing his heart out as they were separated. I know he'd be happy to see them again, that he's been waiting for them all these years."

Her mother smiled. "You just want happy endings these days," she teased.

"Well, of course I do," Maggie said. "I've found mine."

"And Ryan's found his."

"I'm part of it," Maggie agreed. "But he needs his family."

"You know, it wouldn't be so awful if he didn't locate them," her mother said. "He has all of us now and Sean and the Monroes. And Rory and Father Francis. I'd say his life is full."

"He says that, too," Maggie said. "But I want more for him."

"You want it, but does he?"

Maggie thought about it. "Yes, I think he does deep down. Finding Sean was a turning point. Before that, it might not have mattered as much to him, but he's been a changed man since he located Sean." Maggie smiled. "Of course, some of that is because Sean has a wicked sense of humor and a zest for living that can drag Ryan out of his dark moods. I wonder if it was always that way, if Ryan was the serious, responsible big brother and Sean the cutup or if they changed after their parents left."

"You've never asked?" her mother said with a surprised expression.

"They don't like talking about their childhood. Sometimes they'll start, but it always leads back to that day they came home from school and no one was there." Maggie sighed. "Enough sad talk or I'll start crying and have to do my makeup all over again. Have you seen Ryan yet? Is he as handsome as I imagined in his tux?"

"Not as handsome as your father," Nell said with a smile. "But he'll definitely do." She touched Maggie's cheek. "Your father and I want nothing more than your happiness, but I must say I'm thrilled that you've found it here rather than in Maine. It's going to be good having you nearby. We missed you."

"Now I'll be underfoot all the time," Maggie said. "You'll get tired of seeing me."

"Never," her mother said. "And I'm looking forward to all the grandchildren you'll bring over, as well."

Maggie laughed. "Let's not rush things. Ryan's still getting used to the marriage concept."

Her mother glanced at her watch. "Then we'd better not keep him waiting. I'll send your sisters in and then go into the church. Your father's waiting for you in the foyer, probably wearing a hole in the carpet, as he did with your sisters. I love you, Mary Margaret O'Brien."

"And I, you. No woman ever had a better mother."

"And no woman will make a better wife and mother than you," Nell said, tears welling up. "Here, I go again. Let me get out of here."

Maggie's sisters came in as her mother departed

and offered her the traditional something old, something new—a lace-edged handkerchief carried by every O'Brien bride for three generations, a brand-new blue garter from Frannie and a pair of Colleen's pearl earrings, loaned for the occasion.

"I think that's it," Colleen said, standing back to study her. "Mags, you're even more beautiful than I was, dammit."

"But not as gorgeous as I'll be," Katie insisted.

"What an ego, baby sister," Frannie chided.

Maggie laughed. "Come on, guys, let's go march down the aisle and show everyone just how beautiful *all* the O'Brien women are. We'll make Mom and Dad proud."

"They're not proud of us because we're pretty," Colleen began.

"But because we're smart," the rest of them said in a chorus.

Maggie didn't say it, but she thought she might be the smartest one of all, because she'd seen through Ryan's brooding moods and tough demeanor to the wonderful man beneath. And today she was making him hers for the rest of their lives.

"Stop fidgeting," Sean commanded Ryan, "or I will never get this tie on straight! The person who invented these things ought to be taken out and shot. Had to be a woman, since they're the ones always anxious to get a noose around our necks."

Ryan frowned at his brother. "A fine thing to be saying to me on my wedding day."

"Well, it's true. Your Maggie is a wonderful woman, the finest I've ever met, in fact, but making a commitment to her for the rest of your lives requires a kind of courage I can't begin to imagine."

"You're a firefighter, for heaven's sake!"

"I'd risk a burning building a thousand times before saying I do," Sean said with feeling.

"We'll see about that," Ryan retorted. "If I could fall, so can you."

"Never!" Sean insisted.

Ryan laughed. "As an Irishman, don't you know better than to tempt fate that way? The gods are probably up there right this second laughing as they plan your downfall."

Sean shot him a sour look. "Don't go getting any ideas about helping them along."

"Doubt I'll have to," Ryan replied. "Destiny does a pretty good job all on its own."

"Tell that to all the people who meddled in your life to get you to this point."

The door cracked open as if on cue, and Father Francis came in with Rory right behind him.

"Are you thinking of getting married today or next month?" Rory asked irritably, running a finger inside the tight collar of his tux. "I don't know how much longer I can stand this thing."

"Then by all means let's not make you wait," Ryan said, before turning to the priest. "Is Maggie ready?"

"Waiting in the foyer for the wedding march to begin," he confirmed. "And looking like an angel."

Ryan sighed. "Then by all means, let's get this show on the road."

They started from the room, but Ryan caught Sean's arm. "I'm glad you're here to be my best man," he told him. "It makes today feel right."

"From here on out, nothing's ever going to keep us apart again," Sean said, pulling him into a hug. "If the world tangles with one Devaney, it has to deal with both of us. We're a team."

Ryan fought back unexpected tears and forced a smile. "Moving words, but I'm still not sharing Maggie with you. She's mine."

Sean grinned. "No question about that. I've seen the look in her eyes when you're in the room. You'll never have any cause to question her love."

Ryan sighed as a rare feeling of pure contentment stole through him. A ceremony wouldn't change the truth of his brother's words. Maggie O'Brien well and truly loved him.

And that made him the luckiest man on earth.

The ceremony was everything Maggie could have hoped for, though it passed in a bit of a blur. She had a feeling the wedding pictures were going to be disastrous, because one person or another was either bursting into tears or laughing. And the reception at Ryan's Place was filled with music and laughter and dancing.

Through it all Maggie could think of nothing besides the wedding night ahead, which they were spending upstairs before going off on a honeymoon trip to Ireland first thing in the morning. By midnight she was trying to shoo everyone out of the pub.

"She seems a bit anxious for us to leave, don't you think?" her brother Matt asked. "Why is that? It's not as if this night is any different from the others the two of them have shared, now is it?"

"Don't be telling me about that," her father retorted. "Now come along. You didn't find Maggie lingering with you on your wedding nights, did you?"

"Actually, I'm pretty sure she was the one involved in short-sheeting the bed in the hotel on *my* wedding night," John replied.

"Not our saintly Maggie?" Colleen said, feigning shock.

Maggie frowned at the lot of them. "Ryan, as your first official duty as my husband, make them go away."

He laughed. "Aren't you the one who's always telling me about the importance of family?"

She scowled at him. "And it is important, just not tonight."

Her mother finally took pity on her. “Come along, you hooligans. Let’s leave the newlyweds alone.”

Even with that encouragement, it took another half hour to get everyone out of the pub, the doors locked and the lights turned off. When it was all done, Maggie sighed and turned to Ryan.

“Now, then, Mr. Devaney, we are officially on our honeymoon.”

“Is there something special required of me?” he inquired, his expression innocent.

“First you have to carry me upstairs and across the threshold,” she instructed.

When he’d done that, she gazed into his eyes. “Now you have to get me out of this dress.”

He grinned. “With pleasure, though it’s a lovely dress. I could go on admiring it for hours.”

“No, you can’t,” she said. “It’s in the way.”

“In the way of what?”

She touched his cheek. “You making love to me for the first of a million times as my husband.”

“A million times, huh? Won’t I be too worn-out to do anything else?”

Maggie laughed. “Precisely. Which is why I’ll have to take over everything else around here.”

“Is this your devious plan to poke your nose into my accounting ledgers?”

She nodded. “Pretty clever, don’t you think?”

“Come here,” Ryan said, his gaze already heating. “Let’s see how tonight goes, and tomorrow and the day after that. We'll talk again after the five-hundred-thousandth time."

Maggie slipped into his arms. "I can live with that."

"Must be your fine head for negotiating that recognizes a win-win compromise when it's presented," Ryan declared approvingly.

Maggie laughed. "I knew that MBA would be good for something one of these days."

Ryan leveled a long, serious look into her eyes. "You do know I didn't marry you for your MBA, don't you?"

"Why did you marry me—aside from wild, passionate love, of course?"

He touched her face. "Because you're the real family I've needed all my life."

BOOK CLUB DISCUSSION QUESTIONS

1. While Sherryl Woods touches on a number of different issues in RYAN'S PLACE, what is the underlying theme throughout the book?
2. If you have read other books by Sherryl Woods, are there themes or values in RYAN'S PLACE that are consistent with her other work? What are they?
3. Was the book influenced at all by the Boston-Cambridge setting and the Irish background of many of the characters? How might it have been different if it had been set in another part of the country, for example a small town in the South?
4. Ryan's hatred of holidays is one example of how his life has been shaped by his difficult childhood. Were there others? How has your own life been shaped by the things that happened to you as a child?
5. Although we don't yet know why the Devaneys abandoned their three oldest sons to the foster care system while keeping the younger twins, can you think of any excuse that would justify their actions?
6. Do you blame Ryan for not wanting to find his parents or his siblings? Was it inconsistent for him to work so hard to find Lamar's father when he's refused to look for his own?

And once he does begin to search for his family, did you understand his initial need to find an unemotional excuse for finally looking for them?

7. If Ryan eventually does find his parents, what do you think their reaction will be? How do you feel about adopted children searching for their biological parents? What are some of the emotional pitfalls they might face?
8. How difficult do you think it will be for the Devaney brothers to get along once they are eventually reunited? What sorts of issues might they have with each other?
9. When Father Francis reveals Ryan's childhood trauma to Maggie—at that time a virtual stranger—do you feel that his actions were appropriate for a priest? What about his meddling and manipulations to try to bring Ryan and Maggie together? Does it matter that his motives were well-intentioned?
10. What role do you believe fate played in bringing a woman like Maggie into Ryan's life? Do you believe in fate? Are there instances in your own life in which you believe fate had a hand?
11. How about love at first sight? Do you believe it's possible?
12. Though she doesn't call it love right away, almost from the very beginning Maggie

clearly believes that Ryan is going to be an important man in her life. Do you think she was too forward in going after what she wanted from the relationship?

13. Did Maggie's family make it easier or more difficult for her to develop a relationship with Ryan? Have you ever known a family like the O'Briens?
14. The story often talks about counting one's blessings. Are the blessings that touch us always obvious? Can blessings sometimes come from negative events in our lives?

SHERRYL WOODS has written more than seventy-five novels. She also operates her own bookstore, Potomac Sunrise, in Colonial Beach, Virginia. If you can't visit Sherryl at her store, then be sure to drop her a note at P.O. Box 490326, Key Biscayne, FL 33149 or check out her Web site at www.sherrylwoods.com.

Center Point Publishing
600 Brooks Road ● PO Box 1
Thorndike ME 04986-0001 USA

(207) 568-3717

US & Canada:
1 800 929-9108
www.centerpointlargeprint.com